A Christmas Lift

CLARICE JAYNE

Clarice Jype

A CHRISTMAS LIFT

Copyright © 2024 Clarice Jayne

All rights reserved.

The characters and events in this book are fictitious. Any similarity to real persons, living or dead, is coincidental and not intended by the author.

No part of this book may be reproduced or stored in a retrieval system, or transmitted in any form or by any means, electronically, mechanical, photocopying, recording, or otherwise, without express written permission of the publisher.

CONTENTS

	Copyright	iii
	Please Note	Pg 7
	A Christmas Lift Blurb	Pg 9
1	Chapter One – Holly	Pg 13
2	Chapter Two – Nicholas	Pg 22
3	Chapter Three – Holly	Pg 32
4	Chapter Four – Nicholas	Pg 40
5	Chapter Five – Holly	Pg 49
6	Chapter Six – Nicholas	Pg 56
7	Chapter Seven – Holly	Pg 63
8	Chapter Eight – Nicholas	Pg 70
9	Chapter Nine – Holl	Pg 77
10	Chapter Ten – Nicholas	Pg 86
11	Chapter Eleven – Holly	Pg 96
12	Chapter Twelve – Nicholas	Pg 104
13	Chapter Thirteen – Holly	Pg 112
14	Chapter Fourteen – Nicholas	Pg 122
15	Chapter Fifteen – Holly	Pg 133
16	Chapter Sixteen – Nicholas	Pg 142

CLARICE JAYNE

Epilogue – Holly	Pg 149
About the Author	Pg 159
Also from Clarice Jayne	Pg 161

*** Please Note ***

A Christmas Lift

Has been written by an English author in UK English. You may therefore assume there are some spelling errors within it, however, it is just the way we spell things in good old Blighty.

CLARICE JAYNE

A Christmas Lift

Christmas is a time to spend with family and friends. A holiday to be shared. At least, that is for most people.

After a long day at work on Christmas Eve, Holly is on her way home to spend the rest of her birthday and Christmas alone in her apartment. The last thing she expected as she walked into the lift of her apartment building was to end up being stuck in there for hours. Especially with the most gorgeous resident of the building.

Nicholas had just arrived home after visiting his family before they headed off on their Christmas holiday. Resigned to the fact he would be spending Christmas and his birthday alone, he didn't anticipate sharing or being stuck in a lift with the beautiful woman who lived in the apartment across the way.

When a freak accident knocks out the power in the building, Holly and Nicholas are all alone with only emergency lighting and each other for company. Two strangers thrown together on Christmas Eve, awaiting rescue from a stuck lift.

Not exactly a situation that should lead to love. Or could it?

A Christmas Lift is a short holiday romance with a HEA and was originally part of the Gypsy Publishing *Twelve Days of Christmas* Anthology.

A Christmas Lift

CLARICE JAYNE

Chapter One

HOLLY

WHAT A BIRTHDAY I'D HAD.

Having to work until late on Christmas Eve was one thing, but when it was also my birthday, it really sucked. I worked as a legal secretary in a firm of solicitors in the city, and while I really enjoyed the work I did, I hated how much they abused my generosity when it came to staying late to help them with last-minute case notes. It was only when the main partner remembered it was my birthday today at nearly six o'clock this evening that he said I could leave. At least the offices were now closed until the new year and I could enjoy the rest of the holidays.

I had already gotten everything I needed for Christmas Day. It was easy when I knew I would be spending it alone. With both my parents dead and my brother and his family having emigrated to Australia, I always spent my birthday, Christmas, and New Year's on my own. Darren, my brother, always invited me every year to go over and stay with him for the holidays, but I always politely declined. The thought of getting on a plane and flying to the other side of the globe on my own was something I wasn't keen on doing. Plus, the cost of a ticket would be astronomical at this time of year. I always made sure I sent over cards and presents for my niece and nephew and video-called them on Christmas morning to wish them a happy Christmas, even though it was nearly over by the time I called.

So it was yet another lonely Christmas, but to be fair, I liked it that way. I never really liked the whole turkey and trimmings, so, I was just going to have a nice salmon fillet and vegetables for my Christmas meal, with perhaps some mince pies and cream for dessert. The one thing I had forgotten to get was some wine, so I was just going to head into the local supermarket on my way home to pick a couple of bottles of rosé to enjoy over the next few days.

As I walked along the street, there were still plenty of people picking up last-minute gifts and things they had forgotten to buy for the holidays. The walk from my office building to home was always bustling with people, being in the centre of the city, but it always seemed more so at this time of year. The squeals of excited children watching the twinkling lights across the street and rushing to see Father Christmas before he started his long journey to deliver presents sounded along the street. The bitter wind cut through me, causing a shiver to run down my body as I stepped into the supermarket. Immediately, I was relieved to feel the warmth of the heater as I walked through the door.

As I expected, the shop was busy with people getting the last things they needed for the holidays, and I could see it would take a while for me to get the wine I wanted. Walking to the beers, wines, and spirits section, I grabbed the last two bottles of my favourite rosé, Gallo White Zinfandel. Okay, it wasn't the best wine on the market, but for me, it did what I needed it to, and I never drank that much anyway. The two bottles would probably last me way into the new year. I joined the meandering queue to pay for my wine, and twenty minutes later, I was stepping back out into the coldness of the city night.

I pulled the collar of my coat up around my neck to keep the chill off. Even with my thick woollen scarf, the cold was still biting into me. As I walked along the street to my apartment, I watched the people and cars rushing past to spend the holidays at home; I was guessing most were with their families. I felt a slight sadness come over me. Although I liked my own space and tried to convince myself that I preferred to be alone, the truth was, I hated it. It had been ten years since I had spent Christmas with someone else. Ten years since my life had become a lonely one. I had tried dating so many times, but there was something about guys of my age. They just seemed to be out for a good time and didn't want the hassle of settling down. Not that I wanted to marry them immediately and have a family, but I did want a stable relationship. I was nearly thirty. I wanted someone I could rely on, someone to be there for me. I guessed it was why I gave up looking and spent most of my nights working. I didn't have many friends close by. They had all moved away, and most had families of their own now. I guessed I had to resign myself to the fact I would be an old spinster and leave everything to my niece and nephew when I finally left this world.

It was a little over a twenty-minute walk from my work to home, along the busy streets of the city. I briskly walked along the pavement, making my way home, carrying my wine as I walked. The clouds were full of snow, they had said on the weather forecast this morning, so I wanted to get home before it started. I felt the first flake hit my face and the flurry started just as I reached my apartment building.

Pleased in the knowledge that I had made it, I walked through the front door to be greeted by Samuel, the security guard who worked the late shift most days.

"Good evening, Miss Winters. Glad to see you made it before the snow really started to fall. I was getting worried about you."

I loved how Samuel looked out for everyone in the building. He knew every resident by name and made sure to greet them as they walked in the door. Every resident knew that if Samuel was working, they would be safe in their apartments and in the knowledge that no one would get into the building that shouldn't be there. I smiled and walked over to wish him a merry Christmas.

"Merry Christmas, Samuel. Are you working tomorrow night as well?"

A huge smile came across his face, which without saying a word told me he had the night off.

"Not this year, Miss Winters. This year I get to spend it with my family for the first time in a couple of years. Not that we mind. I have to keep a roof over our heads, so we usually celebrate on Boxing Day, anyway."

I watched as he reached down under the front desk and pulled out a box of chocolates and a card.

"You thought I had forgotten you, didn't you? Happy birthday, Miss Winters."

Every year, he did the same. Even if he wasn't working Christmas Eve, I would find a box of chocolates and a card waiting for me at my front door from Samuel and his family. I had made it my business to know the birthdays of all his children and made sure that I got them a small gift and a card each year. I didn't do it to receive; I did it because I knew things were tough for him and his family before he got this job. I wanted them to always have a small gift each year.

"You know you shouldn't spend money on me, Samuel. And will you please start calling me Holly? Miss Winters makes me sound so old."

He continued to smile. "You have looked after me and my family for so long now, it is the least we can do. You know that the girls always remind me a few days before that it is your birthday and that we have to get you a present. They even save up their pocket money each year to buy it. Not that I allow them to pay for it, of course. It is as much for them as me."

How could I deny his sweet girls a little bit of pleasure in their life? The thought of knowing that they remembered my birthday each year, and the fact they offered their own pocket money to pay for it, was so nice and made me feel warm inside. They made me feel like part of their family every year. I knew that I couldn't refuse the gift, knowing how much it meant to them. I took the gift with a smile on my face.

"Thank you, Samuel. And thank Natalie and Sophie for me. Now, I'd best let you get on with your job. Plus, I have a bottle of wine calling out my name."

I held up my shopping bag as I spoke. Samuel chuckled as he looked at the bag.

"Well, you have a lovely evening, Holly. And enjoy your Christmas holidays. I would ask you to spend the day with us, but I know you would only refuse. The offer is there, though, if you want some company."

Another tradition. The invitation to spend Christmas with his family. One that I would never take up. It was meant to be his family time, not inviting a near-stranger into his home. Not that we were really strangers now, but I wouldn't say we were friends either. Just acquaintances.

"Thank you, but no. I wouldn't want to intrude. And before you say a word, I would feel like I was intruding on your family time. You have a lovely Christmas, and I will see you soon."

"You too."

With that, I turned and walked towards the lift, pressed

A CHRISTMAS LIFT

the call button, and waited for the lift to arrive to take me to my floor. Little did I know then what fate had in store for me this evening.

Chapter Two

NICHOLAS

I WAS CURRENTLY SITTING IN MY SISTER, JULIE'S, house with her family and our parents. We were having an early, Christmas as they were all off to Austria this evening to spend Christmas skiing in the Alps. I had been with them for the past two years, but this year I had decided to stay home.

My partnership was in the process of taking over a competitor to save it and the jobs of its workers. The problem was that the employees of the firm of solicitors I was trying to save didn't know what was going on. They had just left to go on their Christmas break happy in the knowledge they would be returning in January, but that might not have been the case if I couldn't pull this off. I couldn't really afford to be away for two weeks, not when we were due to sign all the paperwork in the new year.

Even though I was trying to enjoy my time with my family, my mind kept wandering to work and what I could do to sweeten the deal and make the partners sign over the practice. I was surprised in this day and age that a firm of solicitors was struggling; I knew I certainly wasn't. However, looking at the books and the large bonuses that the partners kept taking out of the company, I was surprised they had lasted this long. I wasn't doing this to save them or line their pockets. I was trying to save the jobs of the staff that deserved to be there and be treated better. The trainee solicitors and admin staff worked their butts off daily to keep the partners in the manner they were accustomed to.

I was pulled from my thoughts when I heard my father calling my name in his booming voice.

"Nicholas Simon Forbes, will you please pay attention?"

My eyes immediately met his when he called me by my full name. I knew I was either in big trouble or had been ignoring my family for a long time.

"I'm sorry, Father. What were you all saying?"

He shook his head with a disapproving look before he spoke to me again.

"If you had been paying attention, you would have realised that your mother was speaking to you. Are you actually with us today or still in the office? It is Christmas, you know."

I hung my head in shame. I knew I should have been paying more attention. But the thought of all those staff was too much for me to forget.

"I'm sorry. I'm just worried about the takeover. I want to make sure all those staff still have a job to come back to after the holidays. I shouldn't let that distract me, though. What were you saying, Mother?"

She gave me a smile as she placed her hand over mine. I knew she would understand if anyone did. She had been in the same situation twenty years ago, and it was thanks to my father that she had kept her job and found the love of her life.

"Nicholas, you care too much about others, but I do understand why. But you need to take some time off for yourself as well. Why don't you come with us for a few days? Even if you come back next week. You know I don't like thinking of you being on your own for Christmas and your birthday."

I knew she meant well and was only looking out for me. But I had already decided that I wanted to spend some time on my own this year. I had already explained everything to my sister, and she understood. I just needed my parents to see it as well. I moved my hand and placed it back over my mother's, giving it a slight squeeze as I spoke.

"I know you are only looking out for me mother, but I will be fine. I'm sure we will speak over the next few days, so I won't be that alone. I just really need to find a way to save the jobs of those poor staff. It's not right what the partners of the firm are doing. They shouldn't be allowed to get away with it, and I am going to do my best to make sure that they don't. You of all people should understand that. And you, Father."

I looked over at him as I spoke and saw the realisation hit his face. He looked directly at Mother before looking at me and smiling.

"We do understand, son. And we know that you will work things out. You know your mother just wants to spend time with you all and make sure you have a good holiday season."

I nodded at him because I did understand. But this was important to me, and I was glad he finally realised how important it was.

"I promise you, once this is all over, we will go on holiday as a family again. Perhaps we could go to Disneyland Paris. I'm sure the girls would love that. I will even be their Prince Charming and take them for a princess makeover."

I knew that Julie had been wanting to take the girls to Paris for ages. But things were tough for them. They only went to Austria each year because my parents paid for them. The girls had wanted to go to Disneyland for ages, and I had promised that I would take them one day, but being a solicitor, things were always busy. But once I had taken over the other partnership, I was going to make sure I made the time to take them.

"Nick, you really don't need to do that. I know how important your time is."

Julie hated accepting anything from me, or my parents. But she always accepted it if it was for the good of the girls, and whether she liked it or not, she would accept this.

"I made a promise to Charlotte and Kirsty that I would take them. You wouldn't want their favourite uncle to look like a liar, now, would you?"

Everyone in the room started to laugh at my comment, and I knew exactly what was coming next before my sister even said it.

"Nicholas, you are their only uncle."

That was the exact answer I expected. I knew I was their only uncle, so I had to be their favourite. I chuckled along with the rest of the family before I answered my sister.

"So that makes me their favourite, then. Come on, I know how difficult things are. Let me give you this. Please?"

I knew she wouldn't let the kids down. In the end, she would agree, and if she didn't, I would just kidnap the girls and take them anyway. She knew I wouldn't take no for an answer and would argue until she gave in. I really didn't know why she even tried; I would always win. She smiled and shook her head in a defeated way. I didn't even let her say a word before I spoke again.

"You know it makes sense, Julie. Now, let's enjoy our short time together before you go zooming down the Alps. I'm already taking bets on who breaks a leg first."

With another eruption of laughter, we all continued to enjoy our time together before it was time for everyone to leave.

The drive home from my sisters to my apartment building was always a slow one, but even more so on Christmas Eve.

With my sister living in the suburbs of the city, it was usually an hour's drive home, but today, it had taken me nearly two hours to get into the city. The Christmas rush of people trying to get last-minute bits and pieces, or rushing home to their loved ones was in progress.

It was just after six-thirty when I pulled into the parking

lot of my apartment building. I placed the code into the keypad and waited for the doors to the underground car park to open. It was one thing I loved about this building: it had a parking space, which was a luxury in the centre of the city. That and the fact it was only a five-minute walk to my office helped. I parked my car in my parking space and headed up to the lobby. There was a lift from the car park directly up to the apartments, but I knew that Samuel was working this evening and I wanted to wish him a merry Christmas before he finished tomorrow morning. I climbed the stairs and entered the main lobby of the building. To my surprise, the young lady who lived across from me was just finishing speaking to Samuel as I walked towards him.

I watched as she walked towards the lifts. I had always liked her, not that I knew her that well. Just a courteous greeting whenever we bumped into each other. I had wanted to get to know her more, but she very much kept to herself. There was something about her, though, that was familiar, and it wasn't that she lived across from my apartment. I was sure I had seen her somewhere else, but for the life of me, I couldn't place her.

I saw Samuel smile as I walked towards him, my mind still thinking about where I had seen my neighbour before.

"Mr. Forbes, merry Christmas. Not staying with the family this year? You are usually on your way to Austria by now, aren't you?"

I smiled at the fact that Samuel knew everyone and knew what they would usually be doing daily.

"Merry Christmas, Samuel. No, I have some business to attend to over the holidays, so I am staying home alone this year. I hope you and your family have a lovely time. Please send my regards to your wife and girls."

I had met his two daughters once while out shopping. They were adorable young ladies, and you could tell that they had been brought up correctly. So polite and sweet, they were a credit to Samuel and his wife.

"I will, Mr. Forbes."

I looked over towards the lift and saw that the doors were just starting to open. I didn't want to have to wait for it to go all the way up to the twelfth floor and then come back down again.

"I'm sorry to rush off, but you know how temperamental the lift can be. I'm going to grab it before the door closes."

Samuel gave me a nod of the head as I quickly walked over to the lift. I promptly spoke to get my neighbour who had already stepped into the lift to keep the door open for me.

"Hold the doors, please."

Chapter Three

HOLLY

I SAID MY GOODBYES TO SAMUEL, THANKING HIM again for my card and chocolates, and headed over to the lift to go up to my apartment. I lived on the twelfth floor.

Each floor had two apartments on it, one on either side. I stood there waiting for the lift to come back down from the top floor. I loved where I lived. It was a nice new apartment building, close to work. I knew that I was always safe here with the security at the main entrance, twenty-four hours a day. And I had the bonus of having a gorgeous neighbour living in the apartment across from mine.

A CHRISTMAS LIFT

I didn't know him that well. I didn't even know his name. But we always acknowledged each other when we met on the landing or in the lobby. So far, I had never seen him when I had been in town or shopping, and up until now we had never managed to share a lift. Little did I know that was about to change. I saw the lift was only a couple of floors away when I heard Samuel greet someone in the lobby. I didn't bother to turn around and see who it was, but I wished I had. The doors opened, and I got into the lift, looking down to press the button for the twelfth floor.

Just as the doors started to close, I heard a voice call out.

"Hold the doors, please."

I quickly looked down to find the button to open the doors again, hearing quick footsteps heading towards the lift. I never understood the difference between the open and close door buttons, I was embarrassed to say. I pressed one of the buttons, only to realise it was the wrong one, when suddenly a hand appeared, forcing the doors to open again, followed by one of the most gorgeous sights I'd seen today: my neighbour. He was casually dressed, telling me that he probably hadn't been to work today, as when I usually saw him, he was wearing a suit most of the time.

As he rushed into the lift, a waft of his aftershave came towards me, and I inhaled deeply as the strong smell of amber and musk hit my senses. It was a smell I would always remember as being the one of the man I had secret desires for. I would never tell him that, I was too afraid of rejection. Plus, he wouldn't be interested in a lowly legal secretary anyway. From seeing how he dressed and presented himself, a model would be far more his type.

I could see it now: a tall – at least five feet, nine inches – thin blonde-haired woman, immaculately dressed, arm in arm with him. Yes, that would be exactly the kind of woman he would go for. Not like me. I had dark hair, a normal size body, was reasonably good-looking, and was five-foot-six. The exact opposite of what I assumed he would like.

As the doors started to close again, I looked up and immediately met his gorgeous brown eyes. He was smiling at me and spoke.

"Thanks. These lifts can be a nightmare, and I didn't fancy waiting for it to go all the way up and back down again."

I smiled back, knowing exactly what he meant. It was the only thing that was annoying about the building. The number of times the lifts were out of action was disgraceful, considering how new the apartment building was. Teething troubles, the contractors always put it down to. But that was no consolation when you had to climb all those flights of stairs to get to your floor. I decided that I would pluck up the courage to speak, rather than just appear to be ignoring him.

"You're welcome. And I understand exactly what you mean. Plus, you never know if it will come back down after going up."

Seeing a slight smirk come over his face, I immediately felt my face heat in embarrassment as I realised the innuendo I had just made. I couldn't believe I had just said that in front of him. I was a complete idiot. He really wouldn't want to know me after a comment like that. His smirk changed to a smile and then a look of concern at my reaction. He smiled at me again and then turned to face the lift doors, so his back was to me.

Some people would have seen this as the height of rudeness, but for me, it was a sense of relief. He obviously saw how uncomfortable I was and decided to try and ease the situation. I stood there allowing my breathing to return to normal. But how could I do that when I now had a perfect view of the back of the Adonis standing in front of me?

I was ingraining every line of his body into my mind. We had never been in this close proximity in the two years I had lived here, and even in our brief moments together, I had never really taken in how fit and muscly he was. I found myself standing there imagining what he looked like underneath his coat. How it would feel to run my fingers across his body. I could feel my heart starting to beat faster, and my breathing shallowed at the mere thought. The butterflies were churning in my stomach and a warmth started to come over me that I had never felt with another man.

I could feel my desire for him growing as I stood there, breathing in his scent. I was sure by now he must have realised that I was staring at him. He could surely feel the heat of my eyes boring into his body. If he did, he never reacted or made a move. He just stood there facing the door without moving. It was only then that I noticed he appeared to be breathing heavily.

Could it be that our closeness was affecting him too? Dare I hope that he had secret feelings for me?

I held back a laugh as I shook my head to erase those thoughts from my mind. I was crazy if I thought he would see me that way. He was obviously a man of means. I was just a humble secretary, nowhere near his standards. He probably owned the company he worked for. If not, he was at least a manager or director.

I took a deep, but quiet breath to calm myself. Looking at the display, I could see that we were on floor seven. Only five more floors to go before this torture was over. The longer I spent near this man, the more I wanted to get to know him and rip his clothes off. I couldn't understand what was wrong with me. I was normally quite a sensible and sedate person, but this man brought out a side of me that I had never felt before. Heck, I didn't even know his name, but I was already wanting to get to know him on a more carnal level.

Could it have been me that was wrong for all these years? Was the idea of just having a fun relationship the way to go, like all my ex-boyfriends had tried to tell me? Was this man in front of me bringing out the side of me that didn't need a steady relationship, just a friend-with-benefits relationship?

No, I couldn't think like that. For one, he wasn't a friend, not even an acquaintance. He was just my neighbour who I said hello to occasionally. Yes, he was drop-dead gorgeous, and every nerve ending on my body was electrified when he was close to me. But I didn't know him. For all I knew, he could be an axe murderer in disguise.

A sudden chill came over my entire body, and I carefully and quietly took a step back to put some more distance between us.

What if he *was* a murderer in disguise? How would I even tell? I could be just standing here and all of a sudden, he could turn on me and murder me on the spot. What the hell was I thinking allowing my thoughts to go so out of control?

A CHRISTMAS LIFT

I was sure he would have tried something long before now if he was a murderer. I started to relax a little and brought my breathing back under control. I took another look at the display, and we were on floor nine. Only three more floors to go before I could escape. Just another few minutes before we were saying our goodbyes and I could go back to secretly lusting over my neighbour without being so close.

A slight flicker of the lights above caught my attention. I felt my heart skip a beat. I hated lifts at the best of times, but I knew it was the quickest way to get to my floor. But the thought of being stuck in here would quickly bring on a panic attack. I looked at the display again and we were still moving, floor ten now. Only two more to go.

Then all hell broke loose. My birthday was turning from bad to worse.

Chapter Four

NICHOLAS

I QUICKLY WALKED TOWARDS THE LIFT AND SAW MY neighbour desperately trying to work out which button to press to keep the lift open. I really didn't understand why they didn't add the words open and close on the buttons, as it would have made it so much easier. As I came up to the doors, they were starting to close. I swiftly placed my hand against one of the doors to kick in the opening mechanism that all lift doors had when they felt an obstruction, and thankfully, the doors started to open again, allowing me access into the lift.

I felt a wave of warmth come over me as soon as I walked in and saw her up close. I couldn't help but smile as she lifted her head from the lift panel and her eyes met mine. I had always had desires for her, even though I hardly knew the woman, and seeing her smiling face only added fuel to the fire I was starting to feel inside. I quickly realised that I had been standing there staring at her for a while, so I thought I would break the tension by thanking her.

"Thanks. These lifts can be a nightmare, and I didn't fancy waiting for it to go all the way to the top and then back down again."

She immediately smiled back at me, understanding. The times the lift had been out of order were terrible considering how new the building was. I had already started legal proceedings against the builders and maintenance company on behalf of all the residents. Perks of being a solicitor and trained in law. I hadn't spoken to anyone yet, as I was hoping to get a settlement out of court. But I had my letter written and ready to deliver to everyone, should they ignore my grievance. It wasn't long before my neighbour replied.

"You're welcome. And I understand exactly what you mean. Plus, you never know if it will come back down after going up."

I couldn't help the smirk that came over my face at her comment. My own thoughts of the gorgeous lady in front of me immediately took over.

I hope it never comes down suddenly came as a reply in my head, but I knew I couldn't say that out loud, especially when I noticed the embarrassment and bright shade of red that was now showing on her face.

She looked so cute when she was embarrassed, but I knew this wasn't helping the situation. I started to feel concerned and worried that my proximity may be intimidating her. After all, I was nearly six-foot-three, and my neighbour was only around five-foot-five, possibly five-foot-six at the most. Deciding to alleviate the situation, I smiled politely, and I turned my back to her. When I pressed the button again for our floor, the lift started its journey again.

As I stood there, I could smell her perfume invading my senses as I started to breathe heavily, affected by her proximity to me. I didn't know exactly what perfume she was wearing, but it was truly addictive. It had a soft floral fragrance with strong citrus notes coming through. It was a smell that I would try not to forget for a long time, as it would forever remind me of her. I could feel my heart starting to beat faster as her presence engulfed me. My breathing became more rapid at the thought of her being so close.

She had caught my attention the first time I saw her. It was the day she moved into the apartment. I had heard the commotion that was going on in the landing one Saturday morning, not long after moving in myself. I had been one of the first residents to move in, but slowly, the rest of the block had started filling up. I went to see what was going on and saw her standing on the landing, directing the removal company on where to put all her things.

I had immediately noticed her hair. Even though it was pulled up into a messy bun, I could see that it was long and thick, and the colour of ebony. Even then, I had wanted to run my fingers through it, and we hadn't even said hello. For someone so dark-haired, her skin was pale, and her lips were red from the harsh cold winter weather. She had reminded me of Snow White, and the phrase "lips red as a rose, hair black as ebony, and skin white as snow" immediately sprang to mind. I had stood there a moment just taking her in, hoping that this could be the start of a beautiful friendship, or maybe even more.

I smiled at her as her eyes met mine and was about to introduce myself when a handsome man around my age came up and flung his arms around her. At the time, I had assumed that it must be her boyfriend or husband, but since that day, I had never seen him again. I hoped that he was just a relative, but since that moment we had never seen each other for more than a few moments.

I had often considered going over and introducing myself to her, but something always held me back. The worry of being rejected always came to mind. I knew I wasn't bad-looking, but for some reason, I always scared women off. I guessed I was just a true romantic at heart who wanted to settle down, get married, and have a family. I thought that was what every woman dreamed of, but it seemed I was out of touch with modern society. Equal rights and all that had changed how some women thought about relationships. Gone were the days of men being studs and women being ridiculed for having one-night stands. Now, it was good for both. That just wasn't me, though, and every woman

I dated seemed to be scared of that.

I looked at the display on the lift, just coming past floor seven. I had been in these close quarters with my neighbour now for a few minutes, and my desire for her was only growing stronger. I wanted to reel around and grab her in my arms. But I knew I couldn't. She wouldn't be interested in me, anyway. I could see her going out with an athletic and well-built guy. Probably with longer blond hair and perfectly tanned. I wasn't small by any means and liked to keep myself toned, but I wasn't what I would call muscular. I was just an average guy that worked as a solicitor.

There was the other problem: my boring job. Well, it wasn't boring to me, but to most, it was. It was on par with being an accountant. No, I would just have to keep my fantasies of the beautiful woman to myself and in the bedroom each evening.

As I stood there, watching the floor display slowly change from nine to ten, I noticed the lights flicker above me. It wasn't an unusual occurrence for this to happen as the lift rose, but something about this time felt different. Something in the pit of my stomach was telling me that something bad was about to happen, and that it was something I wouldn't be able to do anything about.

I was just about to turn and speak to my neighbour when there was a loud noise from somewhere in the building. Within moments, the lift grinded to a halt and all the lights went out, plunging us into darkness.

It was only a few seconds before the emergency lighting came on within the lift, and I quickly pressed the alarm button to get help. I had never really been bothered by lifts or being within enclosed spaces; however, I could still feel my anxiety starting to rise as my heart was beating faster in my chest. I listened as the call went through to the lift maintenance company, and within a little while, a voice came over the speaker.

"This is Martin of the Ascension Lift Company. What is the issue?"

I took a deep breath and answered as calmly as I could, given the situation.

"Hello, Martin. Lift number one in City Way Apartments has broken down. There was a loud noise from somewhere in the building, and then the lift stopped and the lights went out. The emergency lighting is now on, but myself and my neighbour are stuck in the lift. I believe we are somewhere between floor ten and eleven."

I heard him typing at the end of the phone line, making notes on everything I said. He came back within a few moments.

"We have sent for the fire brigade to come out to rescue you. It appears only your block is affected by the power outage, so hopefully they won't be too long. I will call through with any updates I have as I receive them. Please stay calm and try not to panic. We suggest that you sit down on the floor while you wait and try not to move around too much."

"Thank you, Martin. We will wait for an update."

We said our goodbyes, and I went to turn around to speak to my neighbour. All this time, I hadn't noticed what was going on behind me. It wasn't until I turned around and saw how white she had turned that I realised she was having a panic attack. I only had a few seconds to catch her as she started to fall to the ground, shaking in my arms.

Chapter Five

HOLLY

As I stood watching the level indicator slower count through the floors, a loud noise came from somewhere in the building. I watched in horror as the lift was plunged into darkness. I could feel the panic start to set in.

I had always suffered from claustrophobia, thanks to my brother. Darren had always been the practical joker and I remember the day as if it were only yesterday. We were playing hide and seek around the house. I had gone to my favourite hiding spot, which was a small cupboard under the stairs. I hadn't been much older than four at the time, and Darren was nearly seven. He always knew where to find me, as my imagination when it came to hiding spaces wasn't that good. I had been sitting there for about five minutes, happy as usual that he would never find me there, when I heard footsteps coming towards the cupboard. I knew it was him before he even opened the door. I could hear him giggling at the other side.

However, instead of Darren throwing open the door and saying "found you" like he usually did, he locked the door so I couldn't get out.

That was the first of many times that I had a panic attack. I could remember sitting there in the dark and feeling as though the space I was in was closing in on me. Every second, I was being squashed further and further into the back of the cupboard. Even though now I know it wasn't true, I felt as though the walls that I couldn't see were getting closer to me, almost touching me at every moment. It wasn't until my mum walked back in from the garden almost an hour later and heard my screams that I was finally released.

Of course, my brother had thought it was hilarious. However, for me, it had a lasting effect. One that I was very much experiencing now. It was probably only a few seconds before the emergency lighting came on, bathing the lift in a soft glow. To me, it had seemed a lifetime. My anxiety had already risen tenfold, and although I could now see inside the lift and my gorgeous neighbour leaning down and pressing the alarm key, none of this helped. I could feel the sweat starting to build on my skin as my heart rate and temperature started to increase. Like the cupboard, I could feel the walls of the lift closing in on me, trapping me inside this small box that I couldn't escape from.

I could hear a voice coming from somewhere, but I was in too much of a daze to know where from. I just stood there staring in front of me as the pressure of the situation started to build inside me. The walls just got nearer and nearer in my mind. My heart rate continued to rise, and my breathing became erratic. I was struggling to keep my breathing under control as a feeling of intense fear came over me, constricting my chest. The pain I was starting to feel was unbearable and to add to all of this, I was starting to feel nauseous.

I needed to get out of here before it was too late. Before the whole lift collapsed in on itself into a tiny box, crushing me with it. Try as I might, I couldn't stop myself from hyperventilating.

Why hadn't I kept that paper bag in my handbag? I hadn't had a panic attack in years and thought it was safe enough to get rid of it. Was I paying the price for that now?

The more I struggled to breathe, the fainter I was starting to feel. I could feel the dizziness already starting to set in, and I wasn't sure how long I would be able to last on my feet.

The wooziness was taking over my entire body, and I could feel myself shaking as fear started to take over my thoughts. I could feel my legs starting to give way beneath me as I started to collapse onto the floor.

I was too far into my panic attack to realise that I hadn't actually hit the floor. It wasn't until I heard a soft masculine voice next to me that I realised I was currently being held in someone's arms. Then I realised it wasn't someone, but the man I had fantasised about for the past year.

"It's going to be okay."

I looked up to see his gorgeous brown eyes again as he

watched me with a look of concern. I just stood there, feeling his warmth seeping into my body, staring into those eyes. He smiled down at me. I could feel myself stop shaking as the calmness he portrayed to me entered my being. My heart was still beating hard in my chest and my breathing was fast, but slowly, the pain I was feeling started to dissipate.

"Let's get you down on the floor. It's not exactly comfortable, but at least you'll be safe."

He helped me to the floor of the lift and joined me. As he sat next to me, I felt him place his arm around me and rest his hand on my arm, drawing small circles on it. He continued to speak softly to me as we sat there.

"I guess I should introduce myself, as we've never really had the chance before. I'm Nicholas, but you can call me Nick if you prefer."

I couldn't help but giggle when he told me his name. I wasn't sure if it was just because I was nervous, or that I was still getting over the panic of being stuck in a lift. However, it didn't escape my notice that it was Christmas Eve, and I was stuck in a lift with a man called Nicholas. I couldn't help but comment on the situation.

"Well, Nick, it looks as though you will be late delivering presents tonight."

His laughter removed the last hint of worry and panic I was feeling left my body. I was starting to relax as Nick continued rubbing my arm. Finally managing to take a deep breath, I realised that I now knew his name, but I hadn't told him mine.

"I'm Holly, and yes, I have a Christmassy name because my birthday is today. Not that I expected to spend it stuck in here."

I felt Nick squeeze my arm. I couldn't help myself when I leaned into him and placed my head on his shoulder. For the first time in years, I felt safe in a situation like this. The fact that I was stuck in an enclosed space no longer worried me. If Nick was holding me, I knew he would keep me protected.

"Well, Holly, happy birthday. I'm sure it will get better. As for my name, my mother also named me after something Christmassy, because my birthday is on Boxing Day. So, your comment about being late for delivering presents is actually closer than you thought."

I couldn't believe that our birthdays were so close and that our parents shared the same thought when it came to naming us. I started to wonder what else we might have in common.

Chapter Six

NICHOLAS

It hadn't escaped my notice that Holly was now snuggled comfortably into my side, with her head resting on my shoulder. The panic attack she had also been having seemed to be fading, which had been my main concern. I was fortunate not to suffer from claustrophobia, which was what I assumed had brought on her attack, but I could understand exactly what she was going through, as my sister suffered from the same thing thanks to being stuck in a lift for five hours alone.

Having found out that our birthdays were so close together, along with the fact we both had seasonal names, I started to wonder what else we had in common. Could it be that I had finally found a woman who wanted to settle down?

I sat there for a moment, just holding her in my arms, drawing small circles on her arm to calm her. I could hear her breathing start to slow and regulate as she rested on me. I wasn't sure if she was still awake sitting here, so I decided to speak.

"How are you feeling now, Holly?"

I felt her move slightly in my arms before she spoke.

"Much better. Thank you, Nick. I'm sorry I lost it. I have suffered from claustrophobia nearly all my life, thanks to my brother. I guess the lift stopping and being plunged into darkness for a few moments just brought the attack on."

I had guessed right on the reason for the attack, which pleased me, because at least I knew what to do. I gave her a slight squeeze before I spoke again.

"I guessed as much. My sister, Julie, suffers as well. But you are safe here with me, Holly. I won't let anything happen to you."

I felt her relax into me more as we sat there. I wasn't

sure how long we were going to be stuck here, so I thought this could be the ideal opportunity to get to know each other better. She felt so right in my arms that I didn't want to let her go, ever. But we hardly knew one another. I decided that perhaps I should start the conversation going. If anything, it would take Holly's mind off being stuck in an enclosed space.

"I don't know how long we are going to be stuck here, so perhaps we can get to know each other better. After all, we have been living across from each other for the past eighteen months, and today is the first time we found out each other's names."

I felt her chuckle against my chest. It was funny to think that we had been neighbours for so long and had hardly spoken more than two words to each other when we met on the landing. I guessed that was society today. It was a far cry from our parents' time when everyone knew everyone's business. I guessed people just wanted to keep themselves to themselves in this day and age. I thought that to ease her nerves, I would go first.

"I'll go first if you want. As you know, I'm Nicholas, and I am thirty-three years old. I have a sister, Julie, who is two years younger than me. She is married to Roger and has two beautiful daughters, my nieces, Natalie and Sophie. My mother and father are still alive. Both are retired now, but I still ask for his help every now and then."

I felt Holly move slightly so she was looking directly at me as I spoke. A smile on her face as she sat there and listened. Before I could continue, she spoke.

"What do you do?"

I knew this was a risk. Normally when I told someone what my job was, it would immediately cause them to switch off. But I hoped that this time, it would be different. There was something about Holly that was so familiar, as though I had seen her in my business dealings at some point. Taking a deep breath, I continued.

"I warn you it's totally boring."

She laughed again at my statement. It was one of the sweetest sounds I had heard in years, and I wanted to hear it so much more.

What was it about this woman that made me want so

much out of life? I could easily imagine myself in a house, with Holly as my wife and children running around the garden with our family dog. It would be the perfect life for me.

But I couldn't think that far ahead. We had only just met. Love at first sight was never my thing, but I could already feel myself falling hard for this gorgeous woman in my arms, and I still knew nothing about her. I was pulled from my private thoughts by Holly speaking.

"I'm sure it isn't as boring as my job. I'm a legal secretary."

My eyes immediately met hers, and everything started to fall into place. She worked at the solicitor's office I was trying to save. I remembered going there for a late-night meeting, and she was just walking out of the building. It must have been nearly seven in the evening, far too late for a secretary to be working. I had heard they took advantage of their staff, but that was something else.

"Probably more so. I'm a solicitor."

I watched as a look of recognition came over Holly's face. I had probably just blown any chance I had of going out with her, especially when she found out exactly why I had been visiting her boss's practice. The shock in her voice was plain to hear.

"You're Nicolas Forbes, aren't you? I have seen you at the practice I work in. I know something is going on. The partners have been taking as much money out of the business as possible. Am I about to lose my job?"

I could see the worry and anxiety start to build on her face and felt her body tense in my arms. This had been the last thing I had wanted to do. I had calmed her from one panic attack, and I didn't want to be the cause of another one. I gave her a slight smile as I squeezed her into me, trying to give her as much comfort as possible.

"Yes, I am, and yes, something is going on with the partners at your practice. But that is why I have been there. I am trying to save all your jobs. I have a meeting with them next week to finalise everything. I didn't want anyone working there to know until I knew their jobs were safe. But please don't let it concern you, and let's not think about that now. We have enough to worry about, being stuck in here. I promise I will let you know when I have met with the partners."

I didn't want her getting more anxious than she already was, and I knew the situation over her job could tip her back over the edge. I smiled at her before giving her another hug. I felt her relax slightly and hoped that I was putting her mind at ease over both situations.

"Is that why you are still here? I noticed that you usually go away over Christmas and New Year. Well, you did last year anyway."

That comment gave me hope. It meant that she had noticed me as well. How else would she have known that I wasn't there last Christmas? It wasn't as though we saw each other every day. I smiled down at her.

"Yes, it is why I am still here. I spent the day with my family today before they fly off to Austria. They go every year, and I do usually go with them. This year, though, I was worried about everything going on and wanted to make sure it was all finalised before you all go back in the new year. I did have to promise that I would take my nieces to Disneyland Paris in the summer, though. Anyway, I'm sure you've heard enough about me by now. Tell me about you."

Chapter Seven

HOLLY

Being so close to Nick, I could smell the scent of his aftershave even more, and the more I smelled it, the more intoxicating it was. It was almost an addiction. I needed to keep that smell in my senses. It was calming and I was feeling as though I needed it to survive my current ordeal. It was a silly thought, I knew, but Nick had been the only person apart from my mum who had managed to calm me from an anxiety and panic attack.

That was, until I realised exactly who he was. Everyone in the city had heard of Nicholas Forbes and Forbes Solicitors LLP. He was probably the best solicitor in the area, and far better than the partners I worked for. The only reason I was still there was because there were no other jobs around. However, if I'd had the chance, I would have worked for Forbes straight away. I had heard about how they treated their staff, and there was no way I would have been working nearly every night until seven o'clock in the evening and not getting paid for it, or at least getting the time back later when I needed it. But as it was, I was stuck in a dead-end job, with the possibility of being unemployed in the next couple of weeks.

Knowing who he was and recognising him from the practice, though, had brought on the start of another panic attack. I had known something was going on at the partnership. The hushed voices and the letters that I had inadvertently opened were enough to rouse my suspicions. That was how I knew there were no other jobs around, as I had already been looking. Nick had confirmed my worry that the chances were there wouldn't be a job waiting for me when I went back after the holidays.

I felt him pull me into him again and squeeze my arm to calm me. It was almost instantaneous. The calmness I suddenly felt just at his touch. I leaned into him again as he asked me to tell him about myself.

Where did I start? I was nowhere near as interesting as him. I was just a secretary, working every hour I could to keep the roof over my head. And how much longer that roof would be there, I had no idea.

"Come on, Holly. I'm sure there is plenty to tell me about yourself. Just start with your family."

That was, again, where we were different. I had no family in the country, but as he said, it was a good place to start. I took a deep breath before I started to speak.

"I only have my older brother, Darren. Our parents died about six years ago in an accident whilst they were on holiday in Portugal. To this day, we still don't really know what happened. All we do know is one day they were alive, and the next, they were gone."

I felt him squeeze me again as the thoughts of my parents went through my head. It was one reason why I didn't like to talk about my family. I didn't want to remember the fact that I had lost my parents overnight. Again, I felt a warmth come over me as Nick held me in his arms.

"Darren is married to Zoe, and they have two children,

Zara and Henry. They moved out to Melbourne last year. So now it's just me."

It sounded so pathetic when I said it that way. That it was just me. If the truth was known, I liked it that way. I wouldn't have said no to having a man to go home to every evening, but until that man came along, I was happy to live my lonely life.

However, the longer I spent with Nick, the more I wished I could come home to him every evening. I wasn't too bothered about his looks, even though he was gorgeous. It was just his caring nature. I hoped that was him all the time and not just because I had been panicking.

Now it was Nick's turn to speak.

"I'm sorry to hear about your parents. I can't imagine how that feels – only think how I would feel if I lost mine in any way – and I know that I would be devastated."

What I didn't expect was what he asked next.

"I guess you don't go to your brother's because you spend time with your boyfriend over Christmas?"

As he spoke, I could hear what sounded like a jealous tone to his voice, giving me hope that he had some feelings towards me. But then I immediately thought that it was just a question to ask. He would have some beautiful woman to go home to if he wanted to. I was sure of it. Just because I had never seen him with anyone didn't mean he wasn't with someone – girlfriend, fiancée, or even wife. I didn't stand by my door every minute of the day checking.

I realised that I hadn't answered his question when I felt him move around and look into my eyes as though searching for the answer that I hadn't given.

"There is no one else. As I said, it is just me. I spend too much time at work to have any kind of relationship. And anyway, I'm an old-fashioned girl who wants to be swept off my feet by my Prince Charming, settle down, and start a family. There aren't that many men out there that want to do that these days. I guess I will just find myself dying an old spinster, but at least I know I have stuck to my principles. As for going to my brother's, he does ask me every year, but I always decline. The thought of spending so long on a plane, along with the cost, just puts me off. How about you? I'm sure you must have some gorgeous blonde, blue-eyed goddess waiting for you every evening."

I wasn't sure if the look on his face had changed to shock at my last statement because I had hit the nail on the head, or if it was because I couldn't be more wrong. But it was only a few moments before he started to laugh. In fact, he was almost crying before he finally got himself under control and wiped his eyes with his spare hand.

Had I really gotten things so wrong that he could find my comments that funny?

I was sure he must have had someone. I was sure that there were hundreds of women out there that would do anything to get into Nicholas Forbes's bed. If I was honest, I was one of them. But I knew what that would mean. I would just be another notch on the bedpost, and try as I might, I just couldn't do that. No matter how much fun I would have at the time.

As he brought his breathing under control, I saw him shaking his head slightly, possibly in disbelief that I had been so forward in my assumption.

I was about to find out that the truth was far from the assumption I had made of the gorgeous man currently holding me so caringly.

Chapter Eight

NICHOLAS

Hearing about her parents made my heart hurt for her. I couldn't imagine what that felt like, to lose her parents in tragic circumstances without knowing what happened. I'd wanted to wrap my arms around her and take all the hurt away that I could see in her eyes. But a sudden thought came to my mind. I was sitting here with this gorgeous woman in my arms, and I hadn't even considered that she might have a man in her life.

I knew I had to ask, but I wasn't sure I wanted to hear the answer. The more time I was spending with her, even just being stuck in the lift together, the more I wanted to find out about her and spend time with her. All the feelings I'd had over the past year after seeing her for the first time were only growing stronger being next to her.

Her perfume was now intoxicating and taking over all my senses. I wasn't sure if I would be able to think straight for much longer, let alone spend much more time with Holly without taking the kiss that I had been desperate for since I'd walked into this lift. It didn't help when she mentioned that she had no one special in her life. My thoughts went to complete disbelief when she said that she always scared men off because she was an old-fashioned girl who wanted to settle down with someone. She was the woman I had been looking for: one who wanted exactly the same things as I did.

However, what she said next completely stopped me in my tracks.

"How about you? I'm sure you must have some gorgeous blonde, blue-eyed goddess waiting for you every evening."

I looked at her in shock. Was that really the sort of woman that she thought I would go for? She couldn't have been further from the truth. The perfect woman for me was currently in my arms asking stupid questions like that.

I started to laugh. I knew it wasn't the time or the place to lose it like that, but her expectations of my loved one were just so wrong that I couldn't help it. I managed to bring my laughter and breathing under control and squeezed Holly closer to me. I felt her bury her head in my chest even further, as though not wanting to hear the answer I was about to give her.

"I'm sorry for laughing, Holly. I shouldn't have lost it like that. It's just that your assumption of the kind of woman I would go out with couldn't be further from the truth. To answer your question, though…no, I don't have some tall blonde, blue-eyed woman waiting for me when I get home, or anywhere else for that matter. In fact, I don't have anyone in my life."

Without saying a word, I could tell that Holly was shocked to hear that. The sharp intake of breath told me all I needed to know. I thought I would take a chance and tell her exactly what—or who—I was looking for as my loved one.

"I guess I'm just like you. An old-fashioned guy. I want the whole relationship, settling down, and eventually starting a family kind of girl. But I never seem to find those women. The ones who all flock around me are just gold-diggers who just want to be a bit of arm candy on a rich guy's arm. The chances of any of them wanting to start a family are also remote. Heaven forbid they damage their perfect size-eight figures."

I felt Holly move underneath me and looked down to see her looking back at me, with an expression of hope in her eyes. I was sure now that the feelings I had for her were mutual. The smile that was currently on her face and the way she looked towards my lips as though she was as desperate as I was to kiss them, was plain to see. If I was ever going to find out the truth, now was the time.

As much as I wanted to kiss her, I wasn't sure whether it was right to make the first move. After all, we had only really known each other for however long we had been stuck here together in the lift. I decided to continue the conversation where I'd left off not a few moments ago.

"If you want me to be honest with you, the kind of woman I would choose to have in my life would be the perfect snow-white princess who is currently in my arms. But I know that is probably never going to happen. I could never be that lucky. After today, we will probably go back to just saying hello as we pass each other in the hallway."

I could no longer meet her eyes as I spoke. I had opened my heart up to her in such a small space of time. Far quicker than I would have dared to with any other person in the past. Was it just the situation we were in, or was it the fact that I had always wanted Holly in my life? I just waited for the rejection to come. That she would think I was just saying this to make her feel better. To my surprise, though, that dismissal didn't come.

I felt her soft hand rest on my cheek. I closed my eyes as I leaned into it. The warmth radiated through my skin and penetrated my heart. I suddenly felt alive. Like I had finally found the woman I had been looking for the whole of my adult life.

I still couldn't meet her eyes, though. I was worried about what I would see in them, that my admission of how I felt about her would not be reciprocated. It was then I heard her soft and quiet voice.

"Nick, look at me, please."

I took a deep breath and held it for a moment as I slowly opened my eyes and moved my head to face her. It was as she was smiling back at me that I truly noticed how beautiful this woman was. I knew she was gorgeous, but I had never really taken in her features and those stunning hazel eyes that were now looking at me, wet with unshed tears still in them. I hoped they were happy tears and not the tears of a woman about to tell me that she was sorry, but we could never be. I didn't have to wait long to find out.

"You don't know how special and wanted that makes me feel, Nick. I have fancied you since the first day I saw you. I wanted to tell you that the man that ran up to me in such an affectionate way was my brother, especially when I saw the pain and hurt in your eyes. But I guess I never had the courage. I assumed that you would just have gotten on with your life and found a woman you loved. That you wouldn't be interested in a woman like me. I guess we have both wasted the past year when we could have been happy together."

She paused for a moment and smiled before she continued.

"You are the only person who has calmed me when I have had a panic attack, except for my mother. The only man who has cared enough to hold me like this without expecting anything. The only man who wants the same as me."

I wasn't going to wait for another second, realising that she wanted this as much as me. That she had liked me for as long as I had wanted her. I looked down at her rosy-red lips just as she looked at mine. Slowly, I moved towards them. We were going to share our first kiss—the first of many I hoped.

But just as our lips were about to touch, there was a banging above us.

Chapter Nine

HOLLY

I COULDN'T BELIEVE THAT WE HAD BOTH SPENT THE last twelve months hiding our feelings for each other. Our lives could have been so much more had one of us just made the first move, but it had taken us being forced to spend time together stuck in this lift to finally admit it to each other. The fact that he had called me a snow-white princess…I couldn't help but feel as though I had finally found my Prince Charming in Nicholas.

I couldn't help but place my hand on his face after he told me his feelings. Feeling the stubble on his face, I told him my feelings, and he leaned into my touch. When he met my eyes and I saw the lust in them and how he looked down at my lips, I knew it wouldn't be long before we would kiss. I looked into his eyes as he slowly moved his head down towards mine.

This was it. This was when fantasy would become a reality and we would finally kiss.

I closed my eyes as I felt his warm breath on my face. Any moment now, I was going to share my first kiss with Nicholas. It must have been a matter of seconds before our lips were about to touch when we were suddenly broken from our moment with a loud banging above us, and then a voice sounded.

"Hello, are you both okay in there?"

I was both elated and disappointed that our rescuers had arrived. Part of me was glad that we were about to get out of this lift, but part of me wished that I could have enjoyed that moment with Nicholas. That we would have kissed. Now I wasn't sure if it would ever happen. I looked at Nicholas, who seemed to have the same confliction in his eyes. He was the first to speak.

"Yes, we are both fine, thanks."

The voice from behind the door spoke again. "Good to hear. We are about to pry open the door, so you might want to stay back. I'm not sure where you are in relation to floor ten, but we should be able to see soon enough."

I could hear our rescuers trying to open the doors. It sounded as though they were slightly above us, so we must have been just about to reach floor ten when the lift had stopped. I had no idea how long we had been in here and was just about to get my phone out to look when Nicholas spoke.

"It's just past eight o'clock, so we have been in here for nearly two hours. Well, ninety minutes anyway."

I couldn't believe we had been here that long. It had only seemed like an hour at the most, and that was all thanks to Nicholas. I was just about to thank him when the internal doors of the lift started to open and we were bathed in the glow of a flashlight currently being held by one of the firemen who had come to rescue us.

"Give us a moment to make sure the door is propped open and then we can help you out of there. Apologies, it won't be the most ladylike way to get you out, but I'm sure you will understand."

I couldn't help but laugh. Given that we were only

halfway onto the floor, along with the fact that I was wearing a tight pencil skirt, I knew it wouldn't be easy, and there was every chance that Nicholas would see what underwear I was wearing. But now all I cared about was getting out of here.

Nicholas got up from the floor and carefully helped me up too as we waited to be helped out of the lift.

I had to say something to Nicholas before we went our separate ways. Well, at least that was what I expected to happen. Two people thrown together in a close proximity could quite easily fall for each other, but would it continue afterwards? I wasn't sure, so I wanted to make sure Nicholas knew how much he had helped me.

"Nick, before we get out of here, I just wanted to say thank you."

Before I could say another word, I felt his strong arms come around me and pull me into a hug before he spoke.

"You don't have to thank me, and we can talk more once we get out of here. That's if you want to, of course."

I pulled away from him, instantly missing the heat from his body. All I could do was smile and nod my head to confirm that I did want to talk more. Things could have been so different had we been here for just a few minutes more, but now I felt as though I was starting all over again. The voice of the fireman pulled me from my thoughts.

"Right. We are ready here. Miss, would you like to go first?"

I went to pick up my shopping and handbag when Nicholas stopped me.

"I'll pass that up to you in a moment. Let's get you out of here first."

I gave him another nod and made my way over to the door.

"Right, if you could raise your arms, and we will pull you out. Again, apologies for the manhandling, but it's the easiest and quickest way to get you out of there."

I took a deep breath and raised my arms. Suddenly, I

felt myself being lifted up by my waist from behind. Nicholas was being the gentleman again, trying to make it as easy as possible on me. It meant that I wasn't pulled as far as I would have been if I had been on my own, and I was guessing it was far less painful.

I was pulled up through the door and helped to my feet by a young fireman. I was guessing the guy that had been talking to us was in charge and he was there just to help. There were three other firemen at the side of the hallway, and I was carefully passed over to them so they could go and rescue Nicholas.

"Are you okay, miss?"

I looked at one of the men standing in front of me. For some reason, I was now in a daze, the events slowly taking their toll on me. I felt a hand steady me as another dizzy spell came over me. It was nowhere near as bad as before, but it was enough to make me sway slightly as I stood there.

"Miss?"

I looked over at the older gentleman that was now steadying me. "I'm sorry. I just came over a little dizzy. I should be fine in a moment."

I felt him gingerly remove his hand, but keep it in place just in case I went again.

"Just take it easy for a moment. I know you've been through quite a traumatic time. Are you hurt at all?"

I smiled at the fireman and shook my head before I spoke. "No, I am fine. Except for a panic attack, I wasn't hurt at all. Thank you for saving us."

"Just part of the job, miss. We will have your friend out in a moment."

I noticed he called Nicholas my *friend*, as opposed to my boyfriend. I guessed he just wanted to be on the safe side. I watched on as Nicholas handed out my bags and then was helped out of the lift himself. His exit seemed far easier than mine, which surprised me considering our difference in build and weight. I saw him thank the two firemen who pulled us both out, pick up my bags, and then head over towards me.

It was only now that I noticed how dark it was on the landing. I should have known it would be, with only the emergency lighting illuminating the way. As soon as he reached me, he passed me my handbag and then put his arm around me. I felt safe again in his arms. It was like he was my safety net from the world around me, his warmth immediately calming me as soon as I felt it. I thought this feeling would disappear as soon as I was out of the situation, but he still had that effect. I carefully leaned into him, trying not to make my feelings too obvious to anyone around me, including Nicholas. We may have declared our feelings to each other in the heat of the moment, but was that enough to continue now that we'd been rescued?

Nicholas turned to all the firemen that were now standing there looking at both of us. I could feel my face heating slightly at the embarrassment of the circumstances. He thanked all of the firemen again for saving us and then turned to me.

"Come on, let's get you upstairs to our apartments. I'm guessing you don't want to go back in the lift?"

I shook my head vigorously; that was the last place I wanted to be. Nicholas's hand rested on the small of my back, the heat from it penetrating my whole body as he guided me towards the door to the stairs and we headed

A CHRISTMAS LIFT

up to our floor.

Chapter Ten

NICHOLAS

Part of me hadn't wanted to be rescued. All the while we were trapped in the lift together, I felt that a relationship was brewing between us, but now that we were being rescued, I wasn't sure where that would leave us. I stood there and listened to the fire chief explain how he was going to get us out of here. I knew it would be both difficult and uncomfortable for Holly being quite short and the gap up to the door being quite high. I knew there was only one thing to do, and that was to help.

But before I could, Holly stopped and turned to me.

"Nick, before we get out of here, I just wanted to say

thank you."

I didn't give her a chance to say anything further. I just needed to be close to her again.

I pulled her into a hug and quietly spoke to her. "You don't have to thank me, and we can talk more once we get out of here. That's if you want to, of course."

I hoped that she would like to talk more, and I had already decided to invite her in for dinner this evening. Knowing it was her birthday and she was going to spend it all alone, I wanted to make it a special one for her, especially after all we had been through this evening. I was pleased when she smiled and gave me a slight nod. I hoped this meant that we could possibly build a relationship on our trauma, and I was going to give it a damn good try. I stopped her from picking up her bags, as I knew this would only make things difficult for the rescuers, and said I would pass them up in a moment.

Watching her walk over to the lift door, I was right in my thinking that it was going to be difficult for the firemen to help her out, and it could possibly end up with one of them falling in due to how far they had to

reach down. When they asked Holly to lift her arms, I
immediately walked behind her and lifted her by the
waist so she could easily reach the waiting hands of the
firemen.

I watched on as they carefully lifted Holly out of the lift
and to the safety of the landing. I breathed a sigh of
relief that she was finally safe. I knew how much she
had been worried all the time that we were in here and
hoped that my small gestures had helped her. I knew
they helped me. I had finally gotten to know Holly,
something I had wanted to do for the past twelve
months.

I breathed a sigh of relief as I saw Holly being led away
from the open lift door. She was safe. I didn't care
about myself; just knowing that she was out of here was
enough to calm the nerves I had been hiding
throughout this ordeal. Not that being with Holly was
an ordeal, but both of us being stuck in here was. I
picked up her bags and passed them to the waiting
firemen before being helped out of the lift.

As I was pulled up to my feet on the landing, I looked
over to see Holly being supported by one of the

firemen. I could see she looked very unsteady on her feet and wanted to rush over to her. Before I could, though, I was pulled from my thoughts by one of the firemen who had just rescued us.

"Are you okay, sir? Not injured in any way?"

"I am fine, thank you. Thank you for coming as quickly as you could. I know the holidays can be quite busy for you all."

I held out my hand to shake his, which he did, before I continued.

"Do you know what caused the power cut, and is it across the area?"

His face dropped slightly at my question before he proceeded to explain.

"It's just this building that was affected, I'm afraid to say. Well, in some respects it made our life easier that it was only one building, but that doesn't make it better for you and the lovely lady over there."

I looked over at Holly as he said this. She was indeed lovely, and I was hoping to spend a lot of my time with her this evening and from now on. I turned back to the fireman as he continued to speak.

"It would appear that some teenagers got into the car park below and were throwing things around. Luckily, no cars were damaged, but somehow they managed to throw something into the electricity boxes below the building and knocked out the whole building. The electric company is currently there working to fix and restore power, and the police have the teenagers in custody. Luckily, they were not hurt, so there is some good news."

No matter what they had done, and the trouble they had caused, I was happy to hear that they were unharmed. The fact that they were now with the police would hopefully make them think twice about doing it again. I thanked both the firemen again, picked up Holly's bags, and headed over towards her.

She looked far more relaxed and steadier on her feet now than she had a few moments ago. Walking up to her as she looked around at me, I immediately passed her handbag to her and put my arm around her. Something told me that I needed to keep her safe and close to me, that she might be worried, as I was, that what nearly happened in the lift wouldn't happen now we were out. But I was going to make sure it did if I could help it. I instantly felt her lean into me as I held her before she turned to take the shopping bag from me.

"No, I will carry that for you."

I looked at the five firemen who were now all looking at us, I suspected wondering what the relationship was between us. I had to admit I was wondering the same myself, but looking down at Holly and seeing the blush on her face, I figured that it was completely different from the one we'd had this morning. I decided to thank all the firemen one more time for rescuing us.

"I cannot thank you enough for what you have done this evening. Before you say it is your job, I know that, but the fact that you put your lives on the line every day for the people of the city is something that should be remembered, celebrated, and praised every day. So, thank you."

At a chorus of "you're welcome" and "thanks", I turned to Holly and spoke.

"Come on, let's get you upstairs to our apartments. I'm guessing you don't want to go back in the lift?"

I had to laugh at the vigorous way she shook her head. I knew it was a silly statement to make, given her claustrophobia, but I wanted to lighten up the evening after everything we had been through. I placed my hand on the small of her back and guided her towards the stairs. Luckily, as we were now on the tenth floor, there weren't many stairs to climb—only two flights. As we walked up, there was a silence between us, as though neither of us knew quite what to say, but it wasn't uncomfortable. It was just more a time of quiet contemplation, and reflection on the events that had just happened. I opened the door on our floor, and we walked onto our landing and stopped outside our apartments. It was now or never.

"Holly."

"Nick."

We both laughed as we spoke each other's name at the same time. Always the gentleman, I gestured for Holly to go first.

"You go first, Nick. I was only going to thank you for the umpteenth time."

I smiled at her. I would take her thanking me for the rest of our lives if it meant we were together for it. I decided that it was time to ask her to join me for the rest of the evening. This would be the answer to if there could be a relationship between us going forward.

"I was just going to ask if you would like to join me for some dinner this evening? I hate thinking of you spending the night alone, especially with it being your birthday and what happened. It won't be much, but I could use the company."

Seeing her face light up was a picture, along with the smile on her face, which made her eyes almost twinkle in excitement. She was just about to speak when the whole landing was bathed in light as the electricity was restored in the building. I laughed and spoke.

"Well, that was pretty good timing. At least I can actually cook you something now. So, how about it? Would you like to join me?"

The smile was still on her face as she replied. "I would

love to, Nick. Thank you so much for thinking of me."

I felt like jumping for joy when she agreed, but I managed to keep myself under control…for now, at least. I guessed she would probably want to get into something more comfortable, so I made a suggestion.

"Why don't you go and get into something more comfortable and then come over? Is there anything you are allergic to that I need to know about? I wouldn't want to add to the events of today."

She laughed before replying. "No, nothing you need to worry about. I might grab a shower as well if you don't mind. I'll be over as soon as I can."

"Take as much time as you need."

She smiled and took the shopping bag that I was still holding from me, turned, and headed towards her front door. I stood there for a moment waiting for her to go into her apartment before I walked into mine.

I had the perfect idea of what I was going to cook. It was quick and easy and could wait until Holly came around. That gave me more than enough time to shower and change into something comfortable. I was hopefully going to make this one of the best birthdays that Holly had, and if I was lucky, one of the best Christmases for both of us.

Chapter Eleven

HOLLY

I COULDN'T BELIEVE THAT NICHOLAS HAD ASKED ME to go to his place for dinner. My heart skipped a beat as he asked me. I hoped it meant that what nearly happened in the lift wasn't just a heat of the moment thing. Perhaps that meant there was a chance for us to be in a relationship.

I had never found a man who wanted the same as me: to settle down and start a family. Nicholas was everything I could dream of in a man. Gorgeous, understanding, would understand the job I did, and wanted a steady relationship as opposed to a one-night stand, or just someone to call when he felt like it.

I couldn't help the smile on my face as I listened to his question, and it was almost a sign from the heavens when the lights came back on just as I was about to say yes. It also made things far easier for Nicholas now, as he could cook something, which he rightly pointed out in his next statement.

"Well, that was pretty good timing. At least I can actually cook you something now. So, how about it? Would you like to join me?"

My smile just wouldn't fade at the kindness and thoughtfulness of this man. "I would love to, Nick. Thank you so much for thinking of me."

I couldn't help but notice that I had thanked him yet again. I had lost count of the number of times I had and was sure he must be getting tired of me saying it all the time. When he suggested next that I should go and get into something more comfortable, I was truly thankful. I had left at seven this morning, and with it being nearly half past eight, I could do with a shower and getting changed. I agreed to go back around as soon as I could, took my shopping bag from him, and headed towards my apartment's front door.

All the while I was opening the door, I could feel the heat of his eyes on me. I wanted to get in as quickly as possible to look at him through the spy hole in my door. I didn't look around as I walked into my apartment and quickly shut the door behind me. Instantly, I turned to look through the spy hole in the door and watched as Nicholas continued to stand there looking towards my apartment.

I saw a smile appear on his face as he turned and made his way into his apartment. My heart was racing in my chest, and I felt giddy with excitement as I placed everything in the kitchen and quickly ran to my room to grab a shower and find something to wear. The shower wasn't an issue, and I had finished that quickly. I had washed my hair this morning and placed it into my trademark messy bun, so I didn't have to worry about that.

No, the issue came when I tried to find something to wear. What did you wear to your neighbour's apartment? I didn't want to come across as too sexy, as though I was begging for him to take me to bed, but also, I didn't want to look as though I couldn't be bothered. After twenty minutes of standing there and trying countless clothes on, I settled for a casual but slightly revealing cold-shoulder top and a pair of comfortable trousers.

I did, however, make sure that the underwear I was wearing was sexy—just in case, of course. Pulling my hair out of the bun, I quickly brushed and styled it into its natural curls and headed out into the kitchen. When I looked at the clock, it was just after nine o'clock. Usually, now I would just be grabbing something out of the fridge and placing it in the microwave. I never really cared for myself when it came to eating and cooking. Well, except for the weekend. The hours I kept at work didn't really allow me to eat healthily. It was either the microwave or grabbing something on the way home. It would be nice to have a home-cooked meal once in a while. Even my dinner for tomorrow was simple, but at least it was fresh.

I grabbed a bottle of wine to take around to Nicholas's and started to head towards the door. Just before I went to leave, I remembered the tub of Ben and Jerry's ice cream in the kitchen. Deciding it would be fun to take it over, I headed back to the kitchen and grabbed it from the freezer. I chuckled to myself as I walked back to my front door. If the ice cream didn't shout out my intentions and thoughts on Nicholas, then nothing would, and there was probably no hope for me.

I closed my door behind me, first making sure I had my key, and headed over to Nicholas's apartment and rang the doorbell. I knew it might take him a little while to come to the door—after all, I wasn't sure if he was cooking or even having a shower—so I was quite shocked when the door opened almost instantly, as if he had been waiting behind it for me to arrive. I smiled at him as our eyes met and we both stood there looking at each other. Realising that neither of us had said a word, I decided to break the silence between us.

"I brought a bottle of wine and some ice cream. I felt funny about coming over and not bringing anything. I wasn't sure what you were cooking, but I only drink rosé wine, and only this one in particular, so I thought it best to bring some along."

I held out the bottle of wine and ice cream and watched as a smirk came over his face. It reminded me of the one that had appeared when I had made the comment about the lift when we'd first spoken earlier that evening. However, this time, I was expecting it. I was hoping he caught the irony of my choice of ice cream and the meaning behind it. His next statement said it all.

"Ben and Jerry's. You have good taste. And I see you've brought my favourite flavour, Netflix & Chill'd. Thank you."

He closed the gap between us, and for a moment I thought he was going to kiss me. Instead, he whispered in my ear.

"I'm sure we will both enjoy that later."

I felt a shiver of anticipation run throughout my body. It didn't help that I could still feel his hot breath on my skin. Slowly, he pulled away from me and smiled again.

"Let me take those from you and put the ice cream in the freezer. You can open the wine while I cook dinner. Follow me into the kitchen."

He took hold of the bottle of wine, along with the ice cream, and started to walk towards the kitchen. The layout of our apartments was the same, so I knew exactly where I was going. I followed him towards the kitchen, my heart still beating fast in my chest as I walked along. Stepping into the kitchen, I saw Nicholas was already placing the ice cream in the freezer. He closed the door and then went to the cupboard to get out two wine glasses. Without turning around, he spoke.

"Take a seat at the table. I hadn't gotten any wine glasses out as I wasn't sure if you would like any after the day you had."

I walked over to the table in the middle of the kitchen and sat in one of the chairs. The table was already laid out. Not only was this guy caring and understanding, and he could cook, but he was also organised. I was also hoping to find out how good he was in bed, but I was getting ahead of myself.

He walked over, placed the glasses on the table, and passed me the open bottle of wine. I hadn't even noticed that he had opened it. I decided to ask what delights we would be eating.

"So, what are you cooking?"

I started to pour us both a glass of wine, while Nicholas went over to the hob and checked whatever was boiling in a large pot. My guess was we were having some form of pasta dish. I really hoped it was because Italian food was one of my favourites. He turned to look at me, smiling as he spoke.

"Prawn linguine, with a tomato sauce. You said you had no allergies, so I figured I would be okay with prawns."

If I wasn't already falling hard for this amazing specimen of a man in front of me, then his cooking skills would surely have done it for me. The fact that I loved Italian, along with seafood, had me almost declaring my undivided love for him.

"Italian and seafood are two of my favourites, so putting them both together has me hooked."

A huge smile came over his face. "Good. Then we will both enjoy it. It's nearly ready, so you won't have to wait much longer."

Chapter Twelve

NICHOLAS

I STARTED TO PLATE EVERYTHING UP AND GOT THE garlic bread out of the oven. I knew they said that you shouldn't really eat garlic if you wanted to seduce a woman—the smell staying on your breath for ages—but as long as both parties were eating it, I really didn't see the problem.

When I opened the door when Holly arrived, I was taken aback by how beautiful she looked. It was the first time I had seen her with her hair down, and I had to admit it was a look that I loved. Seeing the cascades of thick black curls resting on her shoulders made me want to run my hands through them even more. Pair that with the cold-shoulder top and trousers that she was wearing, and she was picture-perfect.

When I noticed the ice cream that she'd brought over, I wondered if she had done it on purpose or if it was just a coincidence. Netflix & Chill'd was my favourite Ben and Jerry's flavour; I hadn't been lying when I'd said that. I just hoped that her thoughts when she chose it were on purpose, because the idea of spending that kind of an evening together was most definitely appealing.

Placing her meal in front of her and the garlic bread in the centre of the table, I sat down to enjoy the meal together.

"Buon appetito."

I saw a smile appear on her face.

"You speak Italian, are gorgeous, and can cook. Are there no limits to your talents?"

I saw her face change as she realised what she had said. Even though we had admitted to having feelings for each other, Holly had never said she thought I was gorgeous. I could she was slightly embarrassed, the blush on her cheeks that made her look so cute appearing. Thinking it best to ignore her comment and change the subject, I spoke.

"That is about the extent of my Italian. I do, however, speak Spanish and French. As for what other talents I have…" I paused for a second. "Well, people say I am good at my job."

I looked at her as I gave her a wink, leaving any form of innuendo that she wanted to take there.

"Don't let the food go cold."

We started to eat in relative silence, each of us enjoying the food and the company, I hoped. When I looked up at Holly, she did look as though she was relishing the meal.

She looked up from her plate and met my eyes, smiling she spoke. "This is delicious. Thank you, Nick. And thanks for inviting me over. I'm not sure I would have been able to relax or sleep this evening without someone to take my mind off what happened today."

I returned her smile. "You're welcome, Holly. It's nice to have some company and someone to cook for in the evening. It can be quite lonely at night, as you probably know."

Seeing the knowing look come over her face, I hoped that this would be the first of many nights that we would be spending together.

We had finished our meal and were currently tidying everything up in the kitchen. I hoped to spend more time with Holly tonight, because I really didn't want the evening to end. Well, not without Holly in my bed, I wished. Hoping to set a relaxing kind of mood, and perhaps enact my thoughts of a "Netflix and Chill" evening, I thought I would make a suggestion. Placing the last of our plates into the dishwasher, I turned to her and spoke.

"Shall we take the ice cream into the front room and share it whilst watching a Christmas movie? That is, of course, if you didn't want to head back to your apartment."

I stopped myself from saying and head off to bed. I didn't want to make it look too obvious what I was hoping for.

"That sounds like an amazing idea. As long as we aren't

going to have an argument as to whether *Die Hard* is a Christmas film, because it is!"

I had to laugh. It was an argument my sister and I had every year. She was adamant that it wasn't, and I always said it was. Add another thing to the list that Holly and I had in common.

"No argument here. It's a Christmas movie. But I was thinking something a little less dramatic. Come on, let's see what we can find."

I went to the freezer and grabbed the ice cream, got two spoons from the drawer, and followed Holly into the front room. I was pleased to see that she chose to sit on the sofa in the middle, which allowed me to sit next to her. I placed the ice cream on the table and sat down next to her. I had already put the fire on in the room, so it felt nice and cosy. It was more for effect than heat. Being in an apartment block, we couldn't have an open fire, which I would have sorely loved, so I had to make do with a fire-effect electric heater, but it did the job just the same.

Picking up the remote, I turned on the TV and found the Christmas channel. To my delight, they were showing one of my favourite Christmas films, *Miracle on 34th Street*, and to make it even better, it was the original. As I went to get the ice cream, I saw Holly's face light up.

"I love this film. It's one of my favourites. Especially the original, although the latest version with Richard Attenborough was good as well."

I passed her a spoon and opened the ice cream. I was surprised when she snuggled into my side as I held the ice cream over to her to take a spoonful. I could feel my heart starting to beat faster as the warmth of her body penetrated my skin.

We sat there in silence for a while, eating ice cream and enjoying the film. This was something I could very much get used to. What I was worried about was the effect this woman was having on me. Soon, it would be plainly obvious, as I felt myself harden just at her being so close.

I tried to regulate my breathing without making things too obvious, taking a spoonful of ice cream where I could. I wasn't sure how much longer I could keep this up before I was throwing the ice cream on the floor, picking Holly up in my arms, and taking her to my bedroom. Her being next to me just felt so right, as though we belonged together and had done it forever. It was Holly who broke the silence between us first.

"I think that's about as much ice cream as I can take for one night. After that gorgeous meal you cooked, I feel quite full. I don't want to overdo it and make myself feel completely stuffed. Got to think of my figure, you know."

I couldn't stop myself from saying the words that immediately came into my head.

"You have a gorgeous body, and still would if you ate ice cream every day. Well, at least to me, anyway."

I heard her sharp intake of breath. I hoped I hadn't just completely messed things up. I wanted to finish what we had so nearly started in the lift and see where it went. I didn't care if it was just a kiss tonight; I would be happy with that. But I needed to know if what I was feeling could go further. Deciding it was now or never, I started to move my head around to kiss her.

I was about to find out exactly what my words had

done, and it took me by total surprise. Before I could react, Holly had moved over, straddled my lap, and smashed her lips against mine.

Chapter Thirteen

HOLLY

I KNEW I WAS BEING FORWARD WITH MY ACTIONS, BUT I was so desperate to kiss Nicholas. Even though I had secretly lusted after him for the past year, I had felt an immediate attraction to him the first time I had seen him when I was moving in. The events of today had only made those feelings and attraction stronger.

As I was sitting there eating ice cream, I could feel the pleasure building inside me, desperate to be released. I wasn't sure how this was going to go, but I was certain that I needed to try. As I pressed down on his lap and felt his hard length beneath me, I knew this was the right thing to do. Either we were just going to share this kiss or I was in for one hell of a night, and I really hoped it was the latter.

Nicholas returned my kiss with as much passion and fury as me, our tongues duelling for dominance as the kiss quickly heated up. I could feel his heart beating hard in his chest, as was mine. Just as I was about to break the kiss, to take the breath that I sorely needed, I felt his arms reach under my legs as he somehow managed to lift me up as he got up from the sofa. My legs automatically wrapped around his waist, and my arms around his neck as I broke away from the kiss, breathing heavily.

I knew exactly where he was taking me, one of the perks of living across the way and knowing the layout of the apartment. Still, I breathlessly asked the obvious question, just to make sure.

"What are you doing?"

I saw the look of lust in his eyes change to a smirk.

"Something I have wanted to do since the first day I saw you, and have been desperate for the whole day. That is, unless you want me to stop?"

That was the last thing I wanted. I needed this man

probably as much as he needed me right now. I had dreamed of this moment for the past twelve months, and now it was happening. There was no way I was going to stop him.

He smiled as he answered the question for me. "I will take your silence to mean I can carry on."

As we got to his bedroom, he pushed the door open with his foot, and in a matter of seconds I found myself on the bed with Nicholas looming over me. His lips crashed against mine again as we both struggled to undress each other as quickly as possible. He pulled away from the kiss and looked down at me, the pair of us breathing heavily, and I guessed his heart was probably beating as hard as mine was in my chest. Nicholas slowly pressed a kiss into the crook of my neck and softly whispered in my ear.

"I think we both need to get naked and then take our time enjoying each other. What do you think?"

I felt a shudder go over me, the expectation of what was about to happen causing ripples throughout my body. At this moment, I would have agreed to anything. I was like putty in his hands.

Breathing heavily, I answered him. "That sounds like a perfect idea."

Smiling, Nicholas carefully got off me and the bed and held out his hand to help me up. Our attempt to get undressed while frantically kissing each other had failed dismally and we were both still fully clothed. But that was about to change. Cupping my face, Nicholas leaned in and pressed a soft kiss against my lips, then ran his hands down my body, across my breasts, and took hold of my top. I couldn't help the small groan that came from my lips as he brushed over my nipples.

I lifted my arms up as he carefully pulled my top over my head and threw it to the floor.

"Fuck, you have an amazing body, sweetheart."

As soon as he finished talking, he slid the straps of my bra down my arms and reached around to undo it, releasing my breasts to the cool air of the room. I immediately felt my nipples harden at the temperature change. To make it worse, he instantly took one into his mouth, nipping and sucking at it, then moving on to the other. I felt my legs starting to turn to jelly as the pleasurable feelings coursed through my body.

"God, that feels so good, Nick. Please don't stop."

As he continued to pleasure my breasts, I felt his hands glide down to undo my trousers. It was only now that he stopped and started to bend down, taking everything with him. He helped me to step out of my trousers and knickers, then stood back up to look at me. If this had been anyone else, I would have felt self-conscious, but there was something about Nicholas that gave me the confidence to stand there and allow him to take me in. I only allowed for a few moments, though, as he was now wearing far too many clothes for my liking.

Taking a step towards him, I returned the kiss he had given me to my neck and whispered in his ear. "My turn."

I ran my hands across his chest and felt the contours of his defined body underneath his t-shirt. Reaching the hem of the shirt, I started to pull it up over his body, seeing his bare chest for the first time. He helped to remove the shirt, as I would have struggled due to his height. As I ran my finger over his bare skin, I heard him take a sharp intake of breath. I started to feel more confident in my actions as I pressed my lips onto his body and heard the moan that came from his lips.

Running my fingers down his body, I hooked onto his sweatpants and boxer shorts and slowly, carefully pulled them down his legs, releasing his magnificent cock, which was now standing proud from his body. It was certainly impressive, and I could feel the saliva forming in my mouth, desperate for a taste. Helping him out of his clothes, I rested on my knees in front of him. I licked my lips as I went to take his manhood into my mouth.

Suddenly I felt two strong arms lift me up and place me on the bed, followed by the man I was desperate to taste.

"Oh, no. You had your turn. I get to taste first."

His voice was gravelly in its tone. Full of lust, need, and want. The kind of voice that would make any woman go weak at the knees. For once, I was glad that I was lying down on the bed, because I would have surely fallen to the floor just at the sound of his voice. I felt his warm breath envelop me as he pressed his lips into the crook of my neck. No man had ever made me feel the way I was feeling right now, without reaching that point of euphoria when I came.

Nicholas was bringing out emotions and feelings in me that were both strange and welcomed. Just the slightest touch from his fingers and lips caused tingles to run through my body, like a spark igniting something inside of me. I felt his lips touch my skin and let out a soft moan as he gently pressed kisses along my collarbone and towards my breasts.

I didn't recognise the woman I was becoming thanks to this man. My whole body was electrified with every touch, and the pleasure that was building inside me felt amazing. I was sure that I would explode as soon as he touched me down there, and I wouldn't have long to find out. He made his way down my breasts, paying special attention to each nipple—which I was sure were now standing erect for him—as he went. I couldn't help but arch my back and close my eyes as he took each nipple into his mouth and ran his tongue around each of them. He then continued across my abdomen and just above my pelvic bone where he rested for a while.

I looked down to find Nicholas looking up at me, asking whether he could continue without saying a word. I couldn't believe the connection we already had, that words didn't need to be spoken to know what we were both thinking, saying, or asking. I expected that would be something that would take months, if not years, to build between a couple. But with me and Nicholas, it just seemed to come naturally.

I smiled down at him and gave him a slight nod to continue. I daren't tell him that this was the first time any man had taken the time to pleasure me first. That he was the first man to ever taste me in this way. I didn't know what to expect when I felt his tongue circle my clit for the first time, but as soon as I felt it, I knew that I wanted more. The sparks of pleasure that went through my body were something that I wanted to feel constantly.

I thought I moaned his name as he continued to nip, suck and lick my now-sensitive bud, but I wasn't sure. My mind was lost to the feelings that were going through me, and I could no longer think straight. Then it was totally blown as, out of nowhere, an orgasm to end all orgasms ripped through me. I was seeing stars like they always described in those romance books, but you never thought were actually real.

I felt two strong arms wrap around me and felt his lips back on the crook of my neck as he held me. Slowly, I came down from my euphoric high, and my mind started to become my own again as my heart started to return to its normal pace and my heavy breathing eased. All the while, Nicholas lay there stroking my arm and gently kissing my neck. When I guessed he thought I was back in the moment, he spoke.

"You are truly breathtaking when you come, sweetheart. I can't wait to experience that feeling around me."

It didn't escape my notice that he had called me "sweetheart" for the second time this evening. Not that I cared. If it meant that I had to hear him call me that for the rest of our lives, I would be happy because that meant we would be together. My body now felt as though it belonged to me again, and my breathing was totally under control. I decided to confess the truth about what he had just done and how it made me feel.

"Can I confess something to you? That is the first time that any man has taken the time to pleasure me. I have never felt so alive as I did in that moment. Thank you." I pressed a chaste kiss to his lips.

Pulling away, he looked at me and smiled. "Then prepare to feel even more alive, because I haven't finished with you yet!"

Chapter Fourteen

NICHOLAS

I couldn't believe that no man had spent any time to pleasure this gorgeous woman below me. Holly was a woman who should have been loved and cherished, not used just for a guy's pleasure. I was going to make sure this evening that she realised what it was like to be with a real man. One who knew how to treat a woman in the bedroom and allowed her to feel what it was like. I knew I might ruin her for any other man that may come after me, but in my heart, I was hoping that would never happen, because I wanted Holly in my bed for the rest of my life and beyond, if she would let me.

As we both lay there, I felt Holly move beneath me. She moved out from under me and pressed me down onto the bed. Looking at her, I saw a smirk come over her face.

"You may not be finished with me, but I know I haven't finished with you. I believe I started something earlier that you stopped me from doing."

She started to press kisses across my body, moving down lower with each touch. Every time her lips touched my skin, I felt a spark of electricity run through my body. I moaned her name as she headed lower and licked the end of my cock. I closed my eyes as she took my length into her mouth whilst gently stroking the bottom with her fingers.

I was in a state of pure bliss as she expertly sucked, licked, and stroked my length. All the while, she never missed a beat, building a rhythm that was sure to have me coming in a matter of no time.

"Fuck, that feels amazing."

Her groan of appreciation vibrated around my cock, and I could feel my balls starting to tighten and my cock swelling as the telltale feelings started to build inside me as I was about to come. She continued her rhythm perfectly, and I knew if she continued, I wouldn't be able to hold myself back.

Breathlessly, I spoke, trying to warn her of what was going to happen. I didn't want to take her by surprise.

"Holly, not that I'm complaining …but if you carry on like that …I'm going to come."

Holly knew exactly what she was doing and what was about to happen, as I felt her smile around my cock and her pace increased. I threw my head back into the pillow as the tingles in my body quickly changed to ecstasy as I came moaning her name. She slowed her pace and ran her tongue over my now-sensitive tip, licking every last drop of cum off my cock.

I lay there for a moment, comprehending what had just happened. Allowing the feelings of joy and belonging to settle in my head. This woman, who I had really only known for a day, had turned my life upside down. I never wanted to let her go. She slowly moved up and lay next to me. I pulled her into my side, and she rested her head on my chest.

I caught my breath and spoke. "That was amazing,

sweetheart. No woman has made me feel the way you do."

I gently drew circles on her arm as I had done earlier when we were stuck in the lift. Something about this woman made me want to cherish and comfort her all the time. I couldn't really explain what she did to me, but it was a strange feeling, one that I wanted to feel every day.

I felt her lips on my chest as she gently kissed me again. I wasn't sure I would ever get used to her tender kisses.

"I'm glad you enjoyed it. I must admit that I did." I felt her smile on my skin after she spoke.

Who knew that the woman next door was such a sexy minx? If I had known all that time ago, I certainly wouldn't have left it this long to find out. I was also going to find out who the kids were that caused all this trouble because I wanted to give them a reward for finally bringing us together. Perhaps it wasn't moral, but if it hadn't been for their hijinks, I may never have gotten to experience this night.

We lay there in silence for a moment, just relishing the

moments we had just shared together. As I lay there, though, there was one thing I still was desperate to do, and I was about to find out that Holly wanted it too. I had meant what I'd said earlier, that I hadn't finished with her yet, especially after what she had just done to me. I needed to feel her enveloped around my cock.

I felt her head move and looked down to see her looking up at me. As I looked at the woman below me, I could still see the look of lust in her eyes.

She smiled up at me and spoke. "Make love to me, Nick. Let me feel what it is like to truly be alive."

I didn't need any further encouragement. I went to reach over to grab a condom from my bedside table. Why I kept a new packet there, I couldn't remember. It had been ages since I had slept with a woman. I guessed like the Boy Scout I was, I liked to be prepared. Before I could open the drawer, I felt her hand press down on my arm. I looked back at her.

"You don't have to use a condom if you don't want to. I'm on the pill, and I was tested not long ago, which was negative. I would really like to feel you inside me. But it is up to you."

I knew it had been ages since I was last with a woman, and like Holly, I had been tested after my last…acquaintance, shall I put it? I was negative as well. I moved my hand back and carefully positioned myself again between her legs.

I leaned down and pressed a kiss on her lips. "Just for clarity, my last test was negative too, and I would love to feel inside you. But tell me if you need me to stop. I never want to hurt you, sweetheart. I would never forgive myself if I did."

I positioned myself at her entrance and slowly pushed inside her. Feeling her heat and wetness surrounding my cock was one of the most memorable moments of my life so far. One that I never wanted to forget. Hearing her gasp and arch her back as I fully seated myself inside of her, I knew that this was going to be an extraordinary night. Her body seemed so responsive to my touch, or any movement I made. We fit together perfectly and were in tune with each other.

Slowly, I pulled out of her and then slid back in. My movements were slow and methodical. I couldn't help the groan I made as I pushed back inside her, feeling her walls flutter around me at every stroke, each time seeming to pull me further and further inside her. I needed to feel her lips against mine, so I slowly leaned down and started to kiss her.

Our kiss wasn't as frenzied as the one that started on the sofa and then ended up here. This time it was slow and sensual. Both of us explored each other and established the boundaries between us. I continued my movements, feeling her start to swell around me. She might have said that I made her feel alive, but I had never felt this way with any other woman in my life.

I could feel that Holly was close to her release, the pulse inside her growing stronger with every thrust of my cock. I wanted her to pull me into that euphoric state again as she had with her lips not long ago. Hearing her soft moans growing louder, I knew that at any moment, she would fall over into the bliss of her orgasm.

"Come for me, sweetheart. Take me over the edge with you. Make both of us feel alive."

With little warning, her orgasm crashed over her as she called out my name in pure pleasure. The pulses around my cock only lasted a few seconds before I followed her into the bliss of two lovers together. I continued to ride through our orgasms, wanting to make them last for as long as possible. Our hearts felt as though they were beating in unison, along with our breaths. As the blissful feeling started to subside and we came down from our high, I looked down at the woman I had fallen madly in love with. She slowly opened her eyes and looked up at me with pure adoration in her eyes.

Leaning down, I pressed my lips to hers. "Thank you, sweetheart. Thank you for letting me experience that with you. It is a moment I will never forget."

I carefully moved off her and lay next to her. I pulled her into my side again and held her as we both caught our breath. I suddenly felt as though I needed to tell her how much that had meant to me, and how much she now meant to me. Taking a deep breath, I decided to speak. I could have been making the biggest mistake of my life, or I could have been starting a beautiful relationship. Either way, I needed to try.

"I know we have both said it before, but I have never felt the feelings I just had with you before. It felt as though we had both known each other forever and that we were meant to be together. I really don't want this evening to finish, and I never want another woman in my bed. Holly, look, I know this is sudden and may be a shock to you, but I love you. I have never been so sure of anything in my life as I am about my feelings for you."

I had said it, and for once, I knew what I was saying was completely true. I loved this gorgeous woman lying next to me. I was almost ready to get down on one knee, propose to her, and drag her down to a registry office next week to get married. I knew it was so soon, but I just couldn't imagine my life without her. I just hoped that she felt the same way.

I lay there for a while, worrying about how she had taken my words and whether she would even say anything. Luckily, I didn't have to wait long before she spoke.

"I'm so glad you said that, Nick. I was lying here wondering how to tell you my feelings too. I have always fancied you, but until today, I would have said it was lust and not love. But the way you have cared and looked after me today, I have fallen head over heels in love with you. And not just because of this evening, but the whole day. Yes, like you, I know it seems too soon, but I can't imagine spending the rest of my life with anyone else but you. I love you too."

Hearing those words spoken to me, I felt both relieved and ecstatic. For once in my life, I was truly positive that I had found the woman I loved, and who loved me. The woman that I would marry and have a family with. I pressed a tender kiss onto her forehead. I could tell that she was exhausted from both the events of the day and our time in bed together this evening. Tomorrow was a new day—be it Christmas Day—and I knew that, for once, I would spend it with the woman I had fallen madly in love with. We both needed rest, so I pulled the duvet over us both and spoke.

"Get some rest, sweetheart. Today has been both traumatic and enjoyable for us both. I hope I turned a bad day into a good birthday for you. Tomorrow is Christmas Day, and if you will let me, I would love to spend it with you."

Feeling her snuggle into me, I felt a warmth inside me. Even though I was in my own apartment, it finally felt like a home for me, not just somewhere I lay my head at night.

Quietly and sleepily, Holly spoke. "I would love to spend the day with you."

I tenderly kissed her again. "Goodnight, sweetheart."

I heard her soft breaths, telling me that she had already fallen asleep in my arms. It didn't take long before I joined her in the realms of sleep and my dreams, which were now a reality.

Chapter Fifteen

HOLLY

IT WAS CHRISTMAS MORNING, THE DAY AFTER MY birthday, when I usually woke up alone and spent the day lounging around the house in my pyjamas feeling sorry for myself.

So, when I woke up this morning and realised that I was still in Nicholas's arms, I was quite shocked at first. It had been a long time since I had slept all night with someone. I wasn't complaining about it; I was loving the warmth of having him next to me.

As I lay there, I thought back to the events of yesterday. The way Nicholas had cared for and comforted me throughout our time in the lift. Then how he had cooked us both a lovely meal. The way he had tenderly treated me throughout the night, and the emotions and feelings he had brought out of me throughout the night. We had made love several times during the night and early this morning, and each time I felt a new sensation within me. He had certainly made me feel alive, euphoric, loved, cherished, and all the emotions in between.

I didn't realise that Nicholas had now woken up and was lying there watching me. It wasn't until he spoke that I realised he was.

"What are you thinking about, sweetheart?"

I jumped slightly at the sound of his voice, causing a small laugh to come from his mouth. Instantly, though, he pulled me into him and tenderly kissed my head.

"I'm sorry. I didn't mean to make you jump. I thought you realised that I was awake."

I smiled and snuggled into him as he held me. I was getting used to feeling him next to me and how tenderly he treated me. I also enjoyed hearing him call me "sweetheart" all the time. None of my other boyfriends had called me by any pet name, and the fact that Nicholas did made me feel even more special. I realised I hadn't answered his original question.

"I was just thinking about the difference twenty-four hours can make. When I woke up yesterday morning, I was looking forward to another hard day in the office and spending my birthday on my own. And look how that turned out."

I felt him carefully pull me around to face him. Seeing his smiling face looking back at me was a sight I could wake up to every morning. He placed his hand on my face, and I immediately leaned into it and closed my eyes.

"I'm hoping you think that it turned out to be an amazing day, because it certainly did for me. And to wake up on Christmas Day with a gorgeous and sexy woman in my bed tops any Christmas present I could ever get. I meant everything I said yesterday, Holly. I love you, and want to spend the rest of my life with you if you will let me."

I couldn't think of anything that I wanted more than to be with Nicholas for the rest of our lives. I know many people would say we were mad. That we had only really known each other for a few hours, so how could we possibly know that we wanted to be together? But as they say, love is strange, and when it truly entered your heart, you knew. I opened my eyes and went to speak, but Nicholas placed his finger on my lips.

"I don't want you to answer that question now. Today, I just want to pamper you and make it one of the best Christmas Days you have had. I may not have a present for you, but I can still treat you. And that starts with my first tradition of the day, breakfast. I hope you like smoked salmon?"

Could this man have been any more perfect if he'd tried? Someone cooking breakfast for me in the morning got my vote every time. And if he was going to treat me to such luxuries as smoked salmon, I was never going to let him go.

"I love smoked salmon. I'd best go over to my place and grab something to wear. I might grab a shower as well."

I was taken aback when he spoke again.

"You will do no such thing. I have a T-shirt you can wear; it will be more like a nightshirt for you. I forbid you to leave this apartment for the whole day. You are going to be pampered as you should be, as a goddess. You know where the bathroom is if you want to grab a shower. However, I thought we may do that together after breakfast."

The way a smirk came over his face as he said the last part and how he waggled his eyebrows at the statement, I couldn't help but giggle. Not only was Nicholas kind and caring, but he was also funny and mischievous as well. Or was that devious? Either way, I loved him for it.

"Okay, I'll admit that sounds far more fun than taking a shower alone. I'll follow you out in a little while."

"Take your time. You can find a t-shirt over in the wardrobe. Choose any one; it will never be washed again." He gave me a quick kiss on the lips and then got out of bed, grabbed a pair of jogging bottoms, and headed out of the bedroom.

I lay there for a moment, just imagining what life could be like for us both in ten years. Would we be still living in one of our apartments? Would we be married? Have started a family?

I laughed at myself. I would never have had these thoughts about my next-door neighbour twenty-four hours ago. Maybe the carnal thoughts of what had happened between us last night, but not about living together.

I got out of bed and headed into the bathroom to do my business, then grabbed a t-shirt from Nicholas's wardrobe and put it on. I hated to admit that he was right: it was like a nightdress on me, but covered enough not to be indecent. Not that Nicholas would complain, I was guessing.

I walked out of the bedroom and headed into the kitchen to find Nicholas busy cooking away at the stove. He must have heard me walk in, because as soon as I entered, he spoke.

"There is coffee ready in the machine there, or I can make you tea if you prefer. Help yourself to sugar and milk if you want it."

I poured myself out a mug of coffee and grabbed one

for Nicholas too.

"I take mine black with no sugar, thanks."

I wondered how he knew what I was doing, so I turned to find Nicholas looking around at me.

"I'm nearly done here. There is juice in the fridge as well, if you would like to get it out."

I placed the coffee on the table and walked over to the fridge, getting out the jug of orange juice that was in there. I sat down at the table and poured us both a glass. I was intrigued to know what we were having for breakfast. I assumed it would be something like scrambled eggs and smoked salmon, as he had mentioned the salmon earlier. I couldn't see what he was doing, so I decided to ask.

"So, what delights are we having for breakfast, then?"

As I was just finishing my statement a plate was put in front of me and it was not what I was expecting. It was far better.

Nicholas sat down next to me and spoke. "Smoked salmon eggs benedict. I will be honest, the hollandaise sauce was ready-made, as I didn't want to make it this morning, but it still tastes good. Don't let it go too cold."

I cut into the perfectly cooked poached egg. This man was everything a woman could want. How he had never found someone to spend his life with before me was beyond me. But I didn't care about that, because he was mine now. His breakfast was delectable, just like the chef, and I was so pleased he had suggested that we shower together, because even I had to admit it would be far more fun than showering alone.

"This is amazing, but you have to let me cook dinner for us both. I can't let you cook all day, especially as you cooked last night as well. Funnily enough, I have some salmon in my fridge that I was going to have for my Christmas lunch. I was never that keen on Christmas dinner."

Nicholas finished his breakfast and smiled at me.

"I said I would pamper you today and treat you like the goddess you are, and that is exactly what I am going to do. With regards to dinner, great minds think alike, because salmon was exactly what I was going to cook too. Now finish your breakfast, because we both have a date with the shower."

Chapter Sixteen

Nicholas

After breakfast, we thoroughly enjoyed our shower together. So much so, we ended up back in bed until early afternoon. We had spent our time making love, resting, and talking. It amazed me how quickly I had fallen for Holly. I knew I often fell for women quickly until realising they only wanted me for two things: the money they thought I had as a solicitor and the sex. But the feelings I had felt before were never as deep as those I felt for her.

We had spoken more about our lives and what we wanted from them. The more we spoke, the more the both of us realised how similar our outlook and expectation of life was. We both wanted to find someone to settle down with and start a family. Both wanted to move out of the centre of the city and find a nice house on the outskirts, closer to the countryside. We even both wanted to get a dog to have as part of our family.

Like Holly, I couldn't believe how different my life could be in just twenty-four hours. Yesterday, all I had been worried about was saving the jobs of several innocent employees working for a group of money-grabbing solicitors. Today, though, I realised just how important it was to save those jobs, because it included the woman I was now madly in love with and wanted to spend the rest of my life with.

Once we had finally gotten up, we spent the rest of the day lounging around the house and enjoying each other's company. I had even allowed Holly to help me cook our lunch—well, more like dinner, as we hadn't actually sat down to eat until after four o'clock. Spending time in the kitchen with Holly gave me a real insight into what daily life would be like together, and I had to admit it was very pleasing. Not once did we get in each other's way, we were that in tune together. I couldn't really comprehend how two people could work together so quickly as a couple.

The day had been amazing, even though we had hardly done a thing. Just spending the day with Holly was enough to keep me happy. We were currently sitting together in the front room, snuggled on the sofa with a glass of wine each and a blanket keeping us both warm. Not that it was cold, but I wanted to feel like I did every year on Christmas Day when I was with my family in Austria.

I had spoken to my parents and sister and introduced them to Holly. They seemed to love her, which I was pleased about. I was sure I would get twenty questions when they got home, but I would be ready for that. As for Holly's brother, Darren, he was far more suspicious of me. I couldn't blame him, though. Holly was his only sister, after all. Plus, she was younger and he was just looking out to protect her. By the end of our conversation, though, he had seemed to come around. Especially after I promised to bring her to Australia sometime in the new year.

I felt Holly gently moving next to me and looked down to find her looking at me. I could tell there was a question on her mind that she wanted to ask.

"What's wrong? I can see you want to ask something, but aren't sure you want to ask it."

A small laugh came from her lips. She was adorable when embarrassed or nervous. I wasn't sure if I would ever get tired of the insecure Holly, although I had to admit that I liked the confident Holly far more. She hesitated for another moment before she spoke.

"Did you mean what you said to Darren about going to see them next year? Or did you just say it to make yourself look good in front of him?"

I could see why she was worried about asking. I could have taken it one of two ways, but knowing Holly as I did now, I knew she was just worried about me and not herself.

"Of course I meant it. If we are going to stay together, and perhaps get married, we will both need to meet each other's families. And after all, with your parents both unfortunately no longer with us, I will need to get your brother's permission to marry you. He is now head of your family. I have more than enough to pay for us to go, if that is what you are worried about. I could fly his entire family over here if needed. I know it has been a long time since you last saw him, so it is as much for you as it is for him."

Seeing the smile come onto her face was all I needed to know it was the right thing to say and do. Our families were important to both of us. I was lucky that mine lived close by and I could spend time with them whenever I wanted to. I wanted her to be able to do that at least once next year, and every year if it made her happy.

"I'm so lucky to have found you, Nick. If it hadn't been for those kids mucking around, we may never have gotten together."

I smiled at her. "That thought had crossed my mind once or twice, sweetheart."

The pair of us sat there and laughed. It was true. If it hadn't been for them, we may never have gotten together. But that was in the past; now the pair of us were just looking to the future.

The rest of the evening was spent watching cheesy

eighties films on TV. Well, to be fair, there wasn't much watching, more glancing occasionally, in between making out. The only time Holly really paid attention was when *Dirty Dancing* came on. I had to admit it wasn't one of my favourite films, a little too chick flick for me, but I still enjoyed watching Holly as she followed it almost word for word.

Looking over at the clock, I could see that it was coming up to nine o'clock. I could feel Holly's content and shallow breathing as she rested her head on me. The past forty-eight hours were probably taking their toll on her, and I could tell if we stayed here much longer, she would be asleep.

Turning to her, I spoke. "Shall we head to bed, sweetheart?"

To my surprise, I saw a smirk suddenly come over her face. It was the kind of look that I had given her so many times when I was about to say or do something, or if I had a plan to put in place. She got up from the sofa and offered her hand to mine. I took it and got up off the sofa. Before I could grab her to lift her up into my arms, she leaned towards me and pressed a kiss into my cheek before she whispered into my ear.

"On one condition, lover boy."

I raised my eyebrows at her use of what I assumed to be my new nickname. She had paid far too much attention to the film earlier. I was sure I would get used to it after a while. After all, I had been calling her sweetheart, as she said, since last night. She pulled away and looked into my eyes before she smiled and continued.

"Tomorrow, it's your turn to be pampered."

With that, Holly immediately turned around, and with the hottest swaying of her hips, walked towards the door, stopping briefly to turn her head, wink at me, and speak.

"Well, are you coming?"

I was going to pass the comment of "not yet," but she had already made her way towards my bedroom. I wasn't going to let her come back and ask twice, so I followed her out of the room and into my bedroom. I had a feeling tomorrow was going to be the best birthday of my life so far. With plenty more to come.

Epilogue

HOLLY

IT HAD TWO YEARS SINCE THAT FATEFUL DAY WHEN I had been stuck in the lift of our apartment building with Nicholas. So much had happened since then.

Nicholas had taken over the partnership that I worked for, as he promised, and saved the jobs of all the staff, including mine. So, they were all now part of the second branch of Forbes Solicitors LLP. The partners at my old partnership may have gotten a nice payday when Nicholas took over, but he'd had an ace up his sleeve. He had reported them to the legal ombudsman and the Solicitors Regulation Authority for the way they had been running their partnership and the work they hadn't done for their clients. The costs, legal fees, and compensation they were required to pay their staff and clients far outweighed the money they had made from the sale of the partnership, and they would never work again. It felt like justice had been served for all the staff.

Everyone at my old partnership was happy. They now had someone they could look up to for the new solicitors and those in training with Nicholas. Everyone was happily working for Forbes, especially when it was announced that everyone would be getting a pay raise to bring them in line with Nicholas's other partnership.

I continued to work at my old branch for a little while, helping to settle the new solicitors into their roles and assisting a couple of Nicholas's partners to set up there. However, I was soon brought over to the main partnership to work there. I was sure it was just so Nicholas could keep an eye on me along with keeping me close. I was grateful that although I would be working in the same building, I wouldn't be working directly for Nicholas. Everyone knew that we were together, and neither of us wanted anyone thinking I was given a job just because of that, so I was working with one of the other partners.

Well, I would have been except for the other changes in our lives. I was now officially Holly Forbes. We had gotten married in December last year and spent our honeymoon in Austria and then Australia. My brother and his family had come over for the wedding and then joined us with Nicholas's family at a massive lodge in Austria. Then we went and spent a little time with them in Australia before spending some time there on our own.

This, of course, led to the second massive change in our life: our son, who had been born in September. We had spoken a lot about what name to give him, and Nicholas wanted to make sure we remembered my father. As luck would have it, both of our fathers had the same first name: Christopher. So, we were spending our first Christmas with our son, Christopher Nicholas Forbes, along with all our families.

We had bought a large house just outside of the city, not too far away from Nicholas' parents. We didn't want to bring up a family in an apartment building and wanted them to have the same home life as we had both grown up with. Nicholas had paid for my brother's family to fly over and stay in a hotel not far away for the whole of Christmas and New Year. After promising both his nieces that he would take them to Walt Disney World in Florida next year when Christopher was old enough to have some memory of it, they agreed that staying at home this year for Christmas would be a good idea.

So, here we were on Christmas Day, spending time with both our families. My birthday had been spent with my brother and his family, and we were going to spend Boxing Day with Nicholas's family, as it was also his birthday. But today was for everyone. We had woken up early, and for once were going to have a traditional Christmas dinner, as everyone would be here. It would be a far cry from the "barbie" on the beach, as Darren quite often had at Christmas. But I wanted our first Christmas together as a family to be one to remember. One like we used to have with my parents. Perhaps that was why, up until now, I had been so anti the whole Christmas dinner and all the trimmings. Because it brought back so many memories of my childhood. But now I could look forward to those memories with my own son and future children.

So, the day started off with a Christmas brunch of

smoked salmon eggs benedict, as it did every year in Nicholas's household, with the kids just having scrambled eggs on toast. Then we were each allowed to open one present. A tradition that was upheld in both my household as a child and Nicholas's. As Nicholas had cooked the brunch, I decided that with the help of the women of the family, we would all work together to cook the Christmas dinner.

I could see both Nicholas and my brother were horrified at this decision, both of them knowing the level of my culinary skills, but after much persuasion, and the promise from both his mum and sister, Nicholas finally handed the kitchen over to us all. I'll admit now that I was a little out of my depth. Okay, truthfully, I was drowning at the idea, but between us, and with the expert tutelage of everyone there, we managed to cook the perfect Christmas dinner, on time and without any catastrophes.

We sat down to eat at around one o'clock in the afternoon and were finished in time to do the one other thing that was a must in my household every Christmas: the queen's speech, only now it was the king that was addressing the nation. As a kid, I used to find this the most boring part of the day, but there was always the promise of more presents and the afternoon film that came after it. However, to my surprise, all of the children were eager to hear what the new king had to say. I guessed, being his first Christmas address, it was important for everyone to be able to say that they had heard it.

The rest of the afternoon was taken up with unwrapping presents, playing with toys, and just spending time together as a family. It was nearly five o'clock in the evening, and I had gone into the kitchen to make everyone a drink. As I stood there waiting for the kettle to boil, I felt a warmth come over me. Turning around, I expected to find Nicholas standing there, but there was no one. My heart suddenly felt full of joy, and I realised that this was what I had missed for so long in my life: my family. I hadn't had a Christmas like this since we had lost our parents all those years ago.

I couldn't stop the tears that fell from my face as I remembered what it was like to have my parents around, and how much I missed them. I looked up and found Nicholas striding towards me with a look of worry on his face.

"What's wrong, sweetheart?"

My tears slowed as soon as he put his arms around me. He always was able to make me feel better and safe just by being there. He wiped away the last of my tears as he waited for me to answer him.

"I'm sorry. I was just thinking about how much I missed having this since my parents died. I guess thinking about them just made me a little upset. I'll be fine in a few moments."

He pulled me back to his chest and hugged me. "I know my parents could never replace yours, but they love you just as much. As do my sister and nieces. I know your parents would have been proud of the woman and mother you have become. I'm sure they are looking down at you now with huge smiles on their faces. Now, enough of this sadness. Let me help you with those drinks."

We took the drinks into our front room, and I took Christopher from my brother, as I could see he was both hungry and starting to get tired. I knew it wouldn't be long before he fell asleep in my arms. His attempt to drink his milk was getting slower and slower as we sat there and talked. Looking down, I saw that he was already asleep. I decided just to sit there a while just in case he woke up and wanted to finish it. I looked at everyone sitting there around me talking with each other. Two separate families united only in marriage, but who seemed to bond as one family. The children played happily together and shared toys, without any arguments.

As I sat there with Christopher asleep in my arms, my husband at my side, and my own—and new—family around me, I knew that I had been blessed. Life for me couldn't have been any better than this, and it was all thanks to some mischievous kids and an evening stuck with my neighbour in a lift. Or as we liked to now call it, our story of a Christmas lift.

A CHRISTMAS LIFT

The End

CLARICE JAYNE

ABOUT THE AUTHOR

Clarice Jayne is an English Author who published her first book Jessica's King in May 2021.

Living in Kent, The Garden of England, with her husband, daughter and dog, she started writing as a hobby when someone suggested she should publish a book. Jessica's King was the outcome.

Clarice writes mystery romances based in the south of England. All of her books include mystery, a little danger, passion, family, and a happily ever-after.

When she is not writing, Clarice works full time in the healthcare industry, drinks copious amounts of coffee and enjoys spending time with her family.

Follow Clarice Jayne on Social Media by visiting https://linktr.ee/ClariceJayneAuthor.

CLARICE JAYNE

ALSO FROM CLARICE JAYNE

KINGS BROTHERS INVESTIGATION SERIES

Jessica's King

Sienna's King

Ashleigh's King

Madeleine's King

Kelsey's King

Abigail's King

Daniel's King

ANGEL DUET

Buying Angel

Angel's Forever

CLARICE JAYNE

S™ AND A™ B™

Falling for My Sweet Saviour

Recovering Love

A Christmas Lift

Printed in Great Britain
by Amazon